My Secrets, Your Lies

N'TYSE

www.urbanbooks.net

Urban Books, LLC
97 N18th Street
Wyandanch, NY 11798

ISBN 13: 978-1-62286-749-3
ISBN 10: 1-62286-749-1

First Trade Paperback Printing October 2016
Printed in the United States of America

10 9 8 7 6 5 4 3 2 1

This is a work of fiction. Any references or similarities to actual events, real people, living or dead, or to real locales are intended to give the novel a sense of reality. Any similarity in other names, characters, places, and incidents is entirely coincidental.

Distributed by Kensington Publishing Corp.
Submit Orders to:
Customer Service
400 Hahn Road
Westminster, MD 21157-4627
Phone: 1-800-733-3000
Fax: 1-800-659-2436

My Secrets, Your Lies

Dedicated to those still struggling and learning how to walk and survive in their truth. You are not alone.

Prologue

Present Day

9/24/2016 (Saturday) 1:21 p.m. A.M.V.P Prod. Day 1
BENEATH MY SKIN DOCUMENTARY TAKE 1
INT. STUDIO - DAY
[N'TYSE] "Quiet on set!"
[SAND] "Hold up, hold up. My nerves. I don't know if I can do this."
[N'TYSE] "It's okay. Just try to relax. Remember why you're here."
[SAND] *Takes a deep breath.*
[N'TYSE] "Donyell, will you please bring Sand some water."
[SAND] *Gulps down the water as the makeup artist blots the sweat from her face.*
[SAND] "All right. I'm ready. But for the record, I'm here to be the voice for those who can't find their own."

I took a deep breath and drifted far back in time, to when it all started. Before I knew it, I was that confused and afraid little girl again.

Even at the innocent age of eight, I had an attraction to females. I was a straight-up tomboy, and I couldn't help checking out the pretty girls from across the blacktop as they hula hooped and shook their butts to made-up cheers and dance routines. I would secretly admire them from afar as I played basketball with the guys. It was during the height of my curiosity that those moments stimulated my imagination. I then discovered the ultimate pleasure and rewards of gym time. My immature hormones would allow me only to like what I saw and wonder about the rest as I watched tennis skirts rock from side to side. When I found myself fantasizing almost every night about my first girl crush, that was when I really started questioning if there was something wrong with me.

It wasn't until I reached high school that the strong attraction and desires that I had always had for girls announced themselves. I was no longer able to control those emotions that tormented my soul and clouded my mind. I went from denying who I was to actually not giving a damn about that box that society tried to force me in, because it was my right to love whom I wanted to love and how I wanted to love. Even after overcoming many struggles, no one could have prepared me for the impact that decision would have on my life forever.

I wasn't your ordinary kind of guy. I had a few assets that turned women on and a few that turned them off. If I should say so myself, I was one sexy motherfucker. I was mulatto, with flawless sandy-brown skin, hazel-colored eyes, and a tight body. I could finesse the panties off any woman, and I had a pretty boy swagger, which some really couldn't understand. I had been called all kinds of things in my life, but I didn't let it bother me, because for once in my life, I was totally comfortable with this body. I no longer sought anyone's permission to be happy, to be me. I wasn't constrained by judgment, and I didn't feel the need to conform to what others believed was "normal." I rebelled against those idiocies.

My moms and pops kicked me out of the house when I was only sixteen years old, barely a sophomore in high school. I was homeless and left with the responsibility to fend for myself. As if I were not their only child, they made me leave with the clothes on my back, the shoes on my feet, and the "dirty mind" I had shamed them with. I had to beg my homies to let me crash at their spot. I figured out real quick who my *real* friends were. My homie Tazjuan had my back no matter what. He would sneak me into his crib late at night, after his t-jones fell asleep, and would hook a nigga up with some leftovers.

Taz would even give me some of his clothes, so that I didn't have to worry about walking around in the same dirty fit every day. I camped out like a fugitive at his spot for about four weeks, until his mom's jealous and insecure boyfriend popped up one night and blew my cover. Dude had been watching her spot for a whole week, expecting to catch her cheating on him with another man, when all along it was just me crashing for the night. Taz's mom ripped both of us a new asshole, then told me she wasn't about to risk her freedom by harboring a minor. She let me stay for the remainder of the night, but the next morning I was back to what I knew best—looking out for my damn self!

It would be a hot minute before I ever spoke to my parents again. While I had made several attempts to reach out to my mom, begging her and my dad to let me come back home, she had told me I was no longer welcome in their house. She'd said that she and my father had been praying that God would have mercy on my soul and that they would continue to pray "the devilish ways" out of me.

"God will heal you, Cassandra," she would tell me repeatedly, right before going into heavy prayer, followed by the scripture. "If you don't stop this foolishness now and ask for God's forgiveness, you're going to hell! Do you understand what I'm saying, Cassandra? Hell!" she had once cried. "You are going against everything your father and I believe in!" She had stopped with her condemning me to hell long enough to catch a short breath and to collect herself. I recalled feeling so helpless in that moment as tears continued to pour down my face. "How could you do this to us? To me!" she'd demanded to know. At that time, I hadn't had all the right words. I hadn't known what she wanted to hear or what she expected to hear, for that matter.

"Mama, this is who I am." I tried to express myself. Tried to explain things that even I was still seeking the answer for, but I would not dare admit that so willingly then. It was easier just to pretend like I knew this masculine person I was evolving into. I began reciting the lines I had overheard someone who looked like me tell another in a disagreement. It was the first thing that came to mind. The first thing I had ever heard that I could relate to.

"This is how I identify—"

"Stop right there! Don't give me that nonsense," she barked. "You're too young to know the difference. This here ain't nothing but a phase, and I rebuke it in the name of the Lord!"

"It's *not* a phase!" I snapped. "I am gay, Mama! Please . . . just accept that your daughter is gay."

"Confused maybe. But you are *not* one of those lesbians!" she yelled.

I remember slapping my tears off my face before the guy who had walked up behind me to use the pay phone could see that I was crying.

"I gotta go now. I'll call you—"

"Don't even bother," she interrupted. "I can't stand seeing you that way."

Her words of repulsion and disapproval still echoed in my soul, ripping me to the core. She had made me feel as though I had some contagious disease. And honestly, I had even begun questioning if indeed that was the case. After all, I was different.

She and my father wanted nothing more to do with me, and they had made that perfectly clear. Even had gone as far as telling the rest of our family not to have any dealings with me. I became the pariah. It was my punishment for walking in my truth and being unafraid to love my way. But every now and then I couldn't help but wonder . . . wonder what would have happened . . . had I denied those feelings . . . had I kept pretending . . . had I just . . . just . . . stop being me. . . .

Tears began to stream down my face. It felt like I had awakened a beast. My wife ran to my side the second someone hollered, "Cut." She held me. Held me close, like a new mother would her newborn baby. "Breathe," she told me. "Let it all out."

My stomach was in knots, and I knew as much as I needed to get my story out, it wasn't going to be easy. The more I thought about my mother, the harder the tears fell.

"It's okay," N'TYSE said, handing me a tissue. When I finally looked up to accept it, not only was she in tears, but so were several other of the crew members. They were right there reliving my journey with me.

Sand

September 17, 2000

"What's up, baby?" I asked once I heard my girlfriend's sexy voice on the other end of the line. I took a pull from the fruity-flavored Black & Mild.

"Hey, boo! Wait, why haven't you left yet?"

"I'm about to walk out the door now."

"All right. I'll see you when you get here."

"Cool. I love you," I slid in.

"I love you too, babe!"

I hung up the phone and headed out of the two-bedroom apartment that I and my stud bro Spliff shared. Rene couldn't stand Spliff. She felt he was a bad influence, but it was my idea to keep our business far away from Rene. Rene knew only as much as I wanted her to know, but on the cool, Spliff and I were both slanging out of that spot. It was known as the trap, but we referred to it as our local office suite. And while my stud bro had no problem with his chick bouncing back and forth between places, Rene was never allowed in there. I wasn't trying to get her caught up like that.

The way our paths had crossed was pure destiny. We were both sixteen and homeless, doing whatever was necessary to survive. I had gotten kicked out, and she was a runaway. Just looking at her, I wouldn't have thought she was even capable of a thing. She looked so innocent, but I knew better than anybody that looks were definitely deceiving.

I was stung by Rene's beauty the moment I laid eyes on her. She was a shortie compared to my five-nine stature. She had smooth amber-colored skin, mesmerizing eyes, silky black hair that fell across her shoulders, and a banging Coke bottle figure. Baby girl had it going on. It didn't take long for me to win her over. We became close friends, and despite all the disrespectful stares we would always get, Rene never felt ashamed or embarrassed to be around me. When I finally told her what the deal was with me, she admitted that she had always felt there was something *different* about me. Her instincts had been right.

About two weeks later, I was pleading with her to go back home.

"The streets ain't for a girl like you," I told her, trying to get her to understand. "Unlike me, you *choose* to be out here like this. Look around us . . . ," I said, pointing to a homeless man pissing in a beer can only a few feet from us, while a nappy-headed base head approached every car that came in our direction, begging for money. That was my reality—not hers. I hated the thought of not being able to see her every day, but I didn't want to see her in that fucked-up situation.

Yet, regardless of how I said it, Rene wasn't trying to hear it. The pain in her eyes was all too familiar. She had begun to really open up to me. Her birth mother had abandoned her when she was only four years old, and her father was an even further distant memory. She had shared how she had been living with her fourth set of foster parents. She had been with them for only six months, but she hadn't been happy there, and she'd become tired of being recycled in the foster system. She had told me that with her seventeenth birthday right around the corner, she would be out of the system and finally free. So it had become even more apparent that we were more alike than different—we were conquerors.

Rene and I were laying our head at different spots every night, but that was about to change. I was already pocket-change hustling, meaning I was barely making enough in a day to feed myself, but now I had to hustle twice as hard to take care of both of us. I started out selling nickel bags of weed, but that wasn't raking in enough ends, not even enough to pay the weekly rate at one of the cheapest, most disgusting motel dumps in the roughest hood in Dallas. That was when I decided to upgrade the product. My supplier fronted me my first major piece of work. The rest, as they say, was history.

I used my key to unlock the door of her apartment. It was technically ours since I paid all the bills, but we had gotten the lease in her name. I lowered my shades to check out how she'd rearranged the furniture since the last time I was over. Rene had great taste and always kept the place nice and tidy. And with the pink fancy curtains peeled back, the sun lit up the living room. I slid my bag off my right shoulder and tossed it onto the couch. I followed that sweet smell of cucumber melon, her favorite lotion, into the kitchen. She was busting suds in her birthday suit. It was a beautiful sight. I crept up from behind, wrapped my hands around her waist, and pulled her closer to me. As I stroked the hardened chocolate of her perky D breasts, I planted tender kisses along the edge of her neck, licking the morning dew from her skin. She moaned seductively, quivering in response to the art of my stroke. She nestled in my embrace before turning around and greeting me with her smile. She knew exactly what I wanted.

"You'll have your pussy," she reassured me, "*after* we finish this homework." She smiled lovingly. Rene kissed me on the lips and led me by the hand to the dining room table, where she had laid out an assortment of snacks.

She picked up a long oversize shirt of mine that was hanging over one of the chairs and put it on. "This way you can concentrate." She chuckled.

"Very funny," I said, grabbing my bag off the couch. I pulled out my textbooks and binder and placed them on the table, beside hers. "I'll be glad when we finish, man."

"Damn, babe. Get a grip. We just started." She laughed, eyeing me strangely.

"Naw, not like that. I'm sayin' look at us. We doing this shit *together*." I held her with my eyes as I took her hand in mine. "My folks thought I wasn't going to amount to anything. But with this . . ." I pointed to the printouts she had superglued to the front of both of our binders. They were homemade GED certificates, and they served as our motivation and a reminder. She had even gone as far as writing our names on them. "With this," I continued, "I get to prove everybody wrong."

She came closer. So close I could feel my jimmy jumping in my pants.

"This ain't about them, Sand. This"—she put her index finger where mine had just been—"is about proving *yourself* right." We allowed her words to marinate for a moment.

I nodded my head and relinquished a smile. "I hear ya, li'l mama."

"Good! Now, let's get to work."

Sand

May 21, 2003

There I stood, trying on my graduation cap and robe. I had accomplished something in my life that I had never thought I would in this life. I had gone from being a high school dropout to actually getting my GED, and now to graduating from community college with an associate of science degree. I was floating on cloud nine.

I removed the cap from my head, fiddling with the braids that dangled across my shoulders. Rene had braided my hair into sectioned cornrows. She normally would do something creative, like have them crisscross or have them in Iversons, and sometimes she'd throw in twists. She'd freak it out real tight, doing whatever came to mind. I couldn't believe I'd let her talk me into letting my hair grow back out. She was determined to see me rock a different look. She parted and greased my scalp every week, conditioning my hair and giving me hot oil treatments to speed up the process.

Rene bought me ten-carat gold diamond studs for my graduation present. She decided to give them to me early so we could go and have pictures taken, something that I had vowed never to do again. She had to beg me and throw in a little something extra for me to finally give in.

Once we arrived at the picture place, I escorted my woman inside. I had avoided this moment so many times after Rene had mentioned it, afraid of how the pictures would come out. I was afraid of what hidden secrets they might reveal or what lies they might tell. I paid the lady for the portrait package that Rene selected. She insisted on having a big-ass picture to hang over the fireplace. I agreed but really didn't care for the idea too much. The Asian gentleman posed us and snapped at the same time. I knew we were dealing with a professional, but I was still leery about how the pictures might turn out.

The last time I had had my picture taken was back in the first grade. The school sent the students home with picture information, including details about dates and purchase prices. My mom was so happy that her baby would finally have some professional pictures taken, that she'd have something more than the snapshots she and Dad had taken of me running around the house, hiding from them and their camera. She had me all dressed up and looking so cute for the big day. I remember her folding a crisp twenty-dollar bill and placing it inside of a yellow envelope.

When I came home from school that afternoon, she was angry and pissed off at what she saw. She had so much disgust in her eyes that she could hardly tolerate looking at me.

"What is this, Sand?" she kept asking me over and over again. "What the fuck is this? Who told you to do this to your goddamned hair?"

It was very clear what I had done. The two pigtails that hung on each side of my head had been purposely sliced off. I had taken the sharpest scissors off my teacher's desk and had cut the dreadful twigs off my head without thinking twice about it. I had then taken a comb from my backpack, combed my hair all back, then slicked it down with lotion and water. The pretty little red ribbons that had been tied around my pigtails were gone, and the ugly barrettes that had hung from my plaits were in the trash.

My mom eyed me up and down, looking at my hair and down at my red- and pink-flowered dress, which I had gotten all dirty from digging up earthworms with the boys.

"Do you know what you look like now?" she asked me. "Do you know what you fucking look like now?" She then hollered at the top of her lungs, making my ears ring. She pulled me by the little hair I had left and dragged my little ass into the bathroom. "Look at yourself, Cassandra Janene Ross. Look at what you did to your goddamned hair." She cursed over and over. "You look like a damn boy now, you hear me? A damn boy!"

She didn't even bother whupping my ass; she left that for my father to do. When he got home, he was so pissed off that he swore up and down he would have killed me if he touched me. I was told to stay in my room and never come back out. When those pictures finally arrived, I can recall my mom ripping the eight-by-ten straight down the middle and trashing the others along with it.

In the days that followed, I walked around the house like a stranger. I was so young and yet so confused about life and the thoughts that teased my young soul. I used to just brush them off and assume they were all natural, until I reached high school. The ninth grade would be when all those entrapped emotions exposed themselves. That was when my glances at women became stares and when being in the presence of one sent a tingling sensation between my legs.

Snap!

The bright flash from the camera temporarily blinded me. I stood up from the chair that I was posted up in.

"It'll be thirty minutes," the Asian man told us.

"You wanna grab something to eat, baby?" I asked Rene, who was touching up her foundation and lipstick.

"Yeah, baby. I'm starving." She continued putting on her makeup as we walked back out front, toward the car.

I was rolling her Chrysler Sebring for the time being, until my ride was finished at the shop. The metallic silvery color shone bright against the rims that I had added on there. My baby's ride was hooked up to the tee. I opened her passenger-side door, and she hopped in, putting on her brown-tinted shades, which matched the outfit she sported. I started the engine, and we drove a block down the street to Williams Chicken.

"What you want, baby?" she asked, trying to retrieve money from her wallet.

"Put that up. How many times am I gon' have to tell you not to pay for anything yourself as long as I'm with you?"

She looked at me with a smile. "All right, hon. Whatever you say. You the boss, baby."

I removed my wallet from my pocket and flipped through the large bills, trying to find something smaller than a hundred. I handed her the smallest thing I could find.

"Fifty dollars? Is this all you got, Sand? You know they may not have change."

"I just want a medium corn fritter," I told her.

She grabbed her purse and stepped out of the car. While Rene was inside, ordering our food, I waited in the car, listening to a mixed CD with nothing but Dirty South music. I had to turn the volume on level one because I had those speakers I had put in thumpin' like a muthafucka.

As Rene was walking back outside with a bag in one hand and a drink in the other, I noticed some guys who were inside suddenly run out.

"Damn, baby got back," I heard the young, immature boys say in unison.

She waved them off like she better had, and hurried to the car. I guessed they couldn't hear the engine running or see me through the mirror tint, so I prepared to get out of the car. Just as I got ready to step out, they headed back inside. I reached over to open the door for Rene, then took the bag out of her hand so she could get in.

"Damn, those young-ass boys," she said as she flopped down into the seat, sipping her soda through a straw. I handed the bag back to her and buckled up her seat belt, then drove off. By the time we got back to Sophisticated Images, the line had gotten longer and more people were waiting to have their picture taken. Rene stood next to me in line, holding me by the arm, anxious to see how they had turned out. I was anxious too but did not let it show.

"Rene and Sand, package C-thirty-four ready," said the cashier, a young black lady, eyeing me in a peculiar way. I was used to stares, but this one was different, sort of an "I wanna get to know you" stare. She watched closely as Rene sorted through the package, looking for any imperfect prints, and I did as well.

"I love these," Rene kept saying while examining each picture thoroughly. I was watching her and the chick from the corners of my eyes. "We'll take them," Rene said.

"All of them?" the cashier said.

"Yes."

We paid ten dollars for the extra proofs that Rene decided to keep and then stepped out of line.

"You left something, sir," I heard the cashier say behind me.

I turned around, knowing she was addressing me. She handed me my receipt and smiled a sly smile while doing it. I returned the gesture and headed for the door.

We headed home, and Rene was eager as ever to get those pictures into the frames she had bought days earlier. I decided to jump in the shower and allow the water to cool me off since it was such a hot and humid day.

It wasn't until I was stripped naked and looking into the full-length mirror in the bathroom that I really saw myself. I wasn't a boy. Never had been. Just had feelings and thoughts like those of a boy. My small breasts and the slit between my legs reminded me of that. That was why I hated being naked in front of other people. The way that I looked on the outside didn't match how I felt on the inside.

I placed everything on the counter that I had in my pockets and almost flipped out when I saw the name Jasmine written in red ink, along with a phone number, on the back of my receipt. My heart was telling me to rip the damn thing up before Rene saw it; then I thought about how fine Jasmine was and talked myself out of that earlier thought. Besides, there wasn't anything wrong with being *friends*.

Sand

Graduation was tight, but the after party my homeboy James threw for me was off the chain. There were so many women and men in one place that you were guaranteed to leave with somebody.

James was an older cat, probably in his late forties. He was the one who had introduced me to the fast money lifestyle. Once I was hired on his payroll, I had to prove that I could get out there and grind just like all the other niggas. Dude was cool, though. We would even hang out, and I definitely didn't offend or intimidate him. There were times when we would kick it like guys and times when I had to show him that just because I had a split didn't mean he was going to treat me like a chick. When we weren't getting money, we would hit the basketball court, the club, and them bones. We were so cold as a team in dominoes that hardly any of the guys would play us for money. That was actually how some of my chump change would roll in. We played for real money. You had to shoot a hundred spot just to sit down at our table.

James wanted to make sure everybody got their drank on. He had trash cans full of beers, and the bar was full of liquor. He had strippers for me and the whole nine.

Rene had been pissed when I told her that James wanted to throw me a graduation party and get me some strippers. The conversation had gone way past heated when she heard that shit.

"Why the hell you gotta have strippers at a graduation party, Sand? Since when do people hire booty dancers to get ass naked for a graduation celebration?"

"Babe, he just want everybody to have a little fun tonight. You trust me, don't you?"

She'd been mad as hell, and I could hear it in her voice, as well as see it in her eyes. She didn't approve of it but was cool after I tossed her a couple of hundreds to go shopping. Money always makes women hush their mouths.

"Well, just this one time," she'd scolded as I followed her around the house, begging for her permission to attend my own damn party.

She finally approved, under the condition that I called her every hour on the hour. "Babe, if you don't trust me, how about you just come with me?" I asked her.

"You already know that's not my type of crowd. I trust you. It's them skanks that I don't trust." Her mind was made up, so I took the agreement and bounced to the cleaners. I gave her no time to change her mind.

I dropped off all my clothes and some of Rene's at Smith's Cleaners. I told the woman working the drive-through that I would need them ready by 6:00 p.m. She agreed that they would be ready and handed me a flyer with coupons attached. I paid her in cash.

The vibration of my cell phone startled me as the phone danced around in my lap. I muted the car system and answered it.

"Hello. May I speak to Cassandra?"

"This is her," I said hesitantly, trying to figure out the male voice on the other end. No one I knew called me by my full name, only those who didn't know me.

"This is Carl, Carl Williams. I'm a friend of your father's. I was asked to inform you that your mother, Ruby Mae, passed away. Breast cancer took her the day before yesterday. The family is asking that you not attend the funeral, but your father just wanted you to know."

My phone dropped from my hands, and my eyes began to flood with tears. I sat in the car, trying to allow my emotions to flow. My mama. The woman who had birthed me. The woman whose eyes I had inherited and whose smile I couldn't hide. My mother was gone. Away from me, away from earth. She was dead. I wasn't sure if the tears that were falling were from the news he had just given me or from him telling me that my family was banning me from her funeral. It took me a moment to get a grip as I laid my head back on the headrest and took out a cigarette to calm down. Deep in my thoughts and questioning whether I had the guts to show up at the funeral, anyway, I decided going through what my family would put me through wouldn't be worth it, after all. Then all those tears quickly dried up when I started having flashbacks of the last time I saw my mama.

I remembered how Ruby Mae slapped the hell out of me and told me she never wanted to see me again. That was six weeks ago, when I showed up at the house with my graduation invitations. She threw her and my dad's invites back in my face.

"Look what you're doing. I don't know you. I don't have any children. My daughter died when she was sixteen!"

I stood there on the front porch, eye to eye with the door that had just been slammed in my face. I cried like a newborn baby that day.

Remembering all that snapped me out of my trance. If I died to her, then she wouldn't miss me at the funeral. My resentment toward her and my father ran deep. I could never forgive them for the way they had treated me. How could a parent disown their child?

I wiped my face with the back of my hands and pretended like that call had never come through. I had my own method of dealing with my pain, and that method was what had got me this far.

By the time I reached James's house, all my homies who had been invited had arrived. Their cars were parked across the front lawn. I went in the house and began enjoying myself. I was mingling with everyone in sight, the ladies primarily. I just wanted to see if I still had it, and I did. I was pulling women to me like a magnet, and some of the fellas started cock blocking and straight up hatin' on a nigga 'cause they couldn't get any play. They even started asking the ladies if they knew I was a woman. Some of the ladies would nod and be like, "Nigga, I know." And some were like, "Nigga, quit lying. That's not a chick. That's a fine-ass dude. That's what that is." I heard one girl say, "I wouldn't care one bit. He, she . . . whatever it is looks too damn good. All I wanna know is, is she taken? Well, then again, fuck that bitch. She walking around here, dancing with all these other hoes, so she gotta be some unclaimed property."

I chilled before I could get myself into trouble. I got on them dominoes and cards. I walked over to the game room, where all the commotion was.

"Who next up?" I hollered.

"You, if you wanna put your money where your mouth is," a youngster by the name of Ray answered.

I took a hundred-dollar bill from my pocket and laid it on the table. I'd seen the three guys at the table up in James's crib before, buying weed from him or just over chilling. I guess they were all underestimating me, because they started cracking jokes about how I was about to lose my hundred dollars to their shit-talkin' asses.

I kept quiet, laughing them off. "House rules still the same?" I asked.

"And you know it. Ten to get in, nickels don't count, back hand man's points, and everybody for they mutha-fuckin' self," the youngster replied.

"Cool." I reached for my seven, then studied them in my hands. First the big six hit the table. Soon after that dominoes were flying. Everybody was concentrating, determined not to lose part of their bill money. The youngster had to be the one to shit talk and try to get everybody fired up.

"Come on, *mamacita*. What you got over there?"

I looked at him like he had lost his damn mind. "My nigga, my name Sand. Call me Sand, or don't call me at all."

"Ha-ha-ha. Damn, my bad . . . Sand. No need to get all feisty on a brotha. Please forgive me," he teased, hoping for someone to join in with him.

I didn't even bother looking up. I laid down my domino, calling fifteen to the point marker. It was the youngster's go. He quickly threw down his, slamming it hard, like he was about to score something. He made all the damn dominoes shake for nothing. But that was the old jailhouse scare tactic that all niggas enforced when playing bones. The next man played, and then the next. It was back around to me.

"Come on. Study long, study wrong," the youngster protested.

I knew what he was doing. But while he was trying to make me lose focus on my game, I had his bigheaded ass in a headlock. I was applying the pressure, and I knew he felt it. He hadn't called shit but ten during the whole game, and I gave him that. I laid down another domino, and then it was his time.

"What that score look like, my man?" He was paranoid as fuck now. He had less than seventy-five on the score-board, and everybody else was in their third house.

"Don't worry, little man. You'll know who won when the game over." Ray started laughing. That young buck knew he wasn't winning, and everybody else was right on each other's toes. That was another house rule. You had to keep up with your own points. Nobody knew what no one else had until the score taker called first fifty or first hundred. You just had to have a good-ass memory and a hell of a thing for quick addition. And that was me.

"Domino," I yelled.

"Man, why the fuck you didn't stop her?" the youngster screamed to his boy.

"I couldn't, man. All I had was this. I had to play that shit."

The guy to my right added his two dominoes.

"Twenty, and that's game!" I hollered. I stood up from the table, picked up my cash, and was about to walk away when I heard another challenger sit down in the spot the youngster had been in.

"Double or nothing, if you think you bad," the new challenger said.

I looked around the room. Everybody was watching from afar, and some had front-row seats. They enjoyed watching muthafuckas lose their money and then walk away, long faced, like they had lost their damn puppy. The music was thumping, cranking me up a little more.

Shit. What the hell? I thought. I had to show 'em who was boss.

"Wash 'em," I said, accepting his challenge. "Pass me a beer somebody." I sat back down in the same chair, and it was on and poppin' all over again.

I looked at my watch, and it was three hours and six hundred dollars later. I quickly called Rene and let her know that I did not forget about her and that I was in the game. She knew how I was about interruptions, so she was cool.

"How much you make, baby?" she asked, already knowing her man would score.

"Six hundred big ones, mama," I replied.

When I hung up with her, James was announcing the names of the strippers in the order they were about to come out. Chocolate Ty, Honey, Fantasy, and Peaches. Now, Peaches had it going on. She did all kinds of crazy shit. She did some shit with her mouth that had all the guys freaking out, including me. She stood up from doing all those floor-dancing tricks and made her way toward me. She had on a navy blue blazer that fit hella tight. You could see that she had no bra on underneath. She had on a short matching miniskirt that was way up her thighs and some see-through glass-like stilettos. She had the schoolgirl role going on. She grabbed my graduation cap, which I had sat on the bar, put it on, and modeled it for me. Her body was outta this world, and her face was beautiful and innocent.

"Are you the one I came to see?" she asked, staring into my eyes, trying to hypnotize me more than I had already been.

"Yeah, that's me, Ma," I said, talking smooth, with finesse.

"Yeah, she the one," my boy James hollered out back, egging her on to do what he had hired her for.

She sat me down in a chair, and before I knew it, hands were on the floor, feet were in the air, and she was upside down in front of me, pussy popping. Her ass was shaking like a violent earthquake, and her titties were flopping all over the place. She removed the blazer and threw it to her feet. She used it to prevent carpet burns as she seductively twirled her ass on the center floor. One of her nipples was pierced, and she had a tattoo of a long-ass tongue reaching out at her nipple ring.

This girl is hella freaky.

"Touch me," she begged. Her head was down below, and she pretended to give me a head job. "Touch me," she said again.

I wanted to so badly, but I didn't want to violate the bond Rene and I had. But I was already violating it. I had the word *lust* written all over my face. I ached to feel every part of her, wanting to introduce myself to her. She was throwing that pussy at me, dry fucking the hell out of my legs and knees. She climbed onto my lap and ground her ass swiftly back and forth to the tempo. The temptation that this yellow bone stallion fed out had won me over. I gave in. I found my hands glued to her ass, bouncing it up and down, back and forth, rocking it with the beat, and my head was in between her breasts. I hoped that she'd jiggle her titties some more. When the song "Grind with Me," by Pretty Ricky, went off, she quickly stood up and gathered all the denominations of bills that had been thrown her way. Everyone was clapping and bragging on her performance, waving me high fives as I passed them by.

I headed toward the bathroom to try to wipe off some of that lipstick and silver glitter that she had left behind on my T-shirt during her exotic lap dance. It was evidence that Rene could use to convict me of cheating on her. Once inside the bathroom, I wet a paper towel, then attempted to wash away the lipstick stain. That didn't work. Now I was walking around with a big-ass smeared red mark that had only gotten bigger and some glitter that had me sparkling like I was the one who was doing the entertaining. So now the shirt had to come off, but I was still flossed down. I had on my white wife beater, blue jean shorts, and my solid white Jordans. I was still dressed to impress and flossed to defrost. Rene had braided my hair going sideways and had added white beads to the ends.

As I was walking out of the hallway bathroom, I heard my girl Chyna holla my name. She was trying to catch up with me. Pushing her way through the crowd. Now

Chyna was what we gal-guys called a stud princess. She did not act or dress like a dude, but she played the part. She dressed so feminine that it wouldn't have even crossed anyone's mind that she was on the other side. And assumptions would get guys nowhere if they were trying to holla or, better yet, get some ass. However, don't get it twisted with the label *stud princess*. There was nothing sensitive or soft about her at all. If her girl talked shit or got outta line, she got bitch slapped with the quickness. She did the shit so fast, no one would see it coming.

Chyna filled the shoes of a man but also walked in heels and miniskirts. She was a force that couldn't be reckoned with. I had heard from people in the streets that she had cut a girl's throat and sliced her tongue for disrespecting her in the presence of another pimp. But more than that, fucking with a nigga after you had been fucking with Chyna was a fat-ass no-no. She wasn't letting no nigga cut in to what she had to create. If she chose to rent out one of her girls or sell them to a pimp, the ho got taxed and so did the pimp. She was money hungry and hit people where she knew it hurt—in the pockets.

Some of them girls Chyna had working for her, she found on the streets of downtown Dallas. She had taken them in, nourished them, trained them, and taught them how to get out there and use their bodies to get what *she* wanted. She educated them on life and the things needed to survive in it. She wrote the book on female pimping and was a natural-born hustler. When people opened their mouths to talk, she already knew what was coming out. She called all the shots and ran all the shows. Her motto was "Once mines, always mines."

If one of her girls tried to leave her, that was her ass. Chyna had to be the one to do the ditching, and she would ditch a girl when she was damn well ready after using her for everything she could get out of her, and that was just all to it. She was the overseer of any drug-related deal and was still capable of street monitoring her women. She had at least a dozen of them trickin' niggas off. Chyna was a dime piece, and she made sure everyone recognized and respected that. Her women had to be dime pieces as well or at least had to have the potential to be molded into one. And nobody got to play with her toys unless they paid or had her permission.

"What's up, pimpin'?" I said as I checked out her attire. She wore a fitted pin-striped suspender pantsuit with a short-sleeved white blouse underneath and a matching hat that had white and black feathers sprouting from the side. She looked like she was in the damn Mafia or something. Her look was dominant and businesslike, which made it easy for her to be perceived as a bitch who was all about her money and hoes. Her sexy hourglass figure was the envy of most women. Her nails were short and well manicured, and she rocked some open-toe sandals that matched her black-and-white hookup. She didn't carry purses, but I was sure that if she did, they would match too. When she opened her mouth to speak, all that could be seen was a mouth full of platinum princess-cut pink diamonds crushed in each one of her teeth, top and bottom.

"Say, Sand, I have a business proposition for you." She was direct and straightforward with her approach. I already knew what time it was. I had to brace myself.

"What's that, Chyna? What you got up your sleeve now?"

"Sand, I got some hoes around the way who are willing to do whatever I ask them to do to get me this paper."

"What you talking about doing? You already got the hood on lock. Everybody knows whose hoes them are on the scene."

She shook her head. "Nah, Sand. I need somebody like you on my team. You see, I know you hungry. And you get down with me, I'm gon' make damn sure you eat. Feel me? I'm talking about expanding my network. Besides, it's too much money in this for me to be getting it all."

I looked at her with a smirk. "You damn right you getting it all." See, I had one thing over Chyna, and that was a business mind. She conducted business on another level. If someone fucked up or off, they got that ass broken in anal, with no lubrication. She didn't care if she had to pay somebody to do her dirty work. Business was business, and she wasn't letting nobody fuck up her shit. Oh, and she didn't bar no dude. Another pimp trying to threaten her wasn't even happening. She had police, detectives, lawyers, and judges who were looking out for her. Everybody was on her payroll. Her uncle was one of the largest dope dealers in Dallas. That was before he got set up. And rumor had it that it was by his own lawyer. I heard he had millions stashed away. But all that's ghost history. If you were caught talking about that shit, you were a suspected snitch, and everyone knew what happened to snitches.

Chyna knew she was the queen bee, and they did too. She had extreme confidence in knowing she owned the women, and that made her feel like she owned the whole fucking world. But I had tapped into her little so-called escorting service a long time ago. I had watched her and had peeked at how she ran things. Idolizing the twenty-seven-year-old, I had critiqued everything she did and had seen all her flaws. She was too wide open, and even though she had hoes on her team, that didn't mean she had down-ass hoes on her team. They just needed somewhere to lay their heads at night, and she provided that, nothing more. I had heard her hoes complaining to other hoes all the time about how they were fed up with Chyna. They were pissed that she was the only one getting money. Some were just plain tired of stripping and working the streets all around but were too afraid to leave her. They would whine to each other but dared not threaten Chyna by leaving, because they knew there would be consequences and repercussions.

I declined her offer and told her I already had solo business projects lined up. She basically needed someone to manage her fuckups and serve as an underpaid sidekick. The truth was, I was on some more shit. I had shit lined up all right. Me and my girl were about to be living large. I gave Chyna some dap to make sure she was cool with me turning down her offer. She gave it back, and then I knew there were no hard feelings.

I walked around James's big-ass condo, which he had been renting since he moved to Dallas. He lived in a two-thousand-square-foot unit by his damn self and swore up and down he couldn't be happier. He told me he had a young piece of meat that would come through on the regular, but to keep her from getting too comfy in his shit, he was paying for her town house across town.

I checked my cell and saw I had seven missed calls from Rene. I quickly called her. "What's up, babe? You a'ight?"

"I'm fine, but what time are you coming home? I miss you."

"I'll be there in another hour or so," I told her. I could tell she was becoming irritated. We hadn't been away from each other for more than just a few hours since I moved in, and she was home alone, missing me like crazy. I adored the thought.

"Well, I wish you'd hurry on up. I'm beginning to feel a little neglected," she purred.

"I'll be there soon," I kept reassuring her. We hung up with "I love yous," and I walked back into my party.

Peaches was giving James and Spliff a table dance, and two other strippers had joined in. The party was getting real crunk, and everybody was having fun. I posted up at the bar and poured me a glass of vodka. The DJ slowed the party down again with R. Kelly's "12 Play." And again the hunt was on.

I grabbed a fine-ass girl who was right in front of me. I had a drink in one hand and was trying to twist her around toward me with the other. She backed her ass up to me real slow and sexy like. When she turned around, my face dropped and my hazel eyes went squint. I was sure that the smoke from the weed and the cigarettes that were being puffed on all night had affected my vision. To my surprise, there stood a caramel-colored woman with an out-of-this-world body, in a sexy net piece. I had seen the woman before. If it hadn't been on the streets, it had been in my dreams. Then I remembered. It was her. The chick who had slipped me her number at Sophisticated Images.

She smiled, watching me as I stood there, shocked and in disbelief. She continued to dance, her body rocking to the beat. I was grinding on her ass, imagining what she had on under that net. I was trying to behave myself, but I was gon' let my imagination run as wild as it wanted to. I pictured her wearing a sheer thong with a matching lace bra. I was trying like hell to see all that her net was exposing. She had her hands up in the air and was sliding up and down on me to the music, swaying that ass like a belly dancer. I was enjoying every minute of her show. I looked around the room, and everyone on the dance floor was coupled up with somebody. Some of the men had them a woman, and some of the studs had theirs. Everyone was having a nice time.

Jasmine was hot. Her short hair was slicked all back, unlike the time I had seen her at work, and she was rocking some small gold hoop earrings. At that moment she had all my attention. I grooved with her until R. Kelly went off and H-Town came on. The DJ sure was trying to get some shit started up in here tonight. I could feel it. Jasmine and I shared a secret vibe. She kept on dancing, allowing the music to get her loose, while I was still sippin' on my drink and rubbin' on that ass.

Sand

My mind had been blown away from the night be-fore. The drinks had got to me so bad, I could hardly remem-ber what all went down. I let the warm water streaming from the showerhead slap me in the face. Images kept fucking with me and creeping into my mind as I replayed last night. I remember Peaches, and I damn sure could recall Jasmine, and I remembered the guest bedroom.

I shook off the possibilities and pretended that what I was sure had gone down had not happened. I didn't even know these women that well. How could I be so stupid? I wanted to slap the shit out of myself until I bled. I wanted to feel some sort of pain. I didn't even care if it was self-inflicted and on the suicidal edge. I wanted to ram my head into the shower glass and cause myself some serious head damage. I wanted to grab one of Rene's razors from under the cabinet and cut my wrists. I felt so stupid.

I had betrayed the one woman who had stood by my side. The woman who had always stuck by me through hard times.

She had endured being made the laughingstock at work and being humiliated every day just for being in love. She had never just come out and said she was gay. Then one day they had seen me drop her off at work. We had smothered each other with wet, long kisses before she could get out of the car good. It had taken only one guy to become the rumor starter.

Rene already knew her coworkers thought she was gay, because she would respectively decline her boss's passes at her. She would tell him she was involved with someone, and when they never saw anyone else take her to and pick her up from work every day, they knew it had to be me. I wasn't ashamed of who I was, but I sometimes felt that I was robbing Rene of the opportunity to discover her own sexuality.

I eventually made her quit that job so I could take care of her. I wanted to prove to her that I would never leave her side and that she could count on me because I was worthy. She was my energy, my air. I thought about all the good times we had shared and everything she had ever sacrificed. Everything I loved and admired about her and our relationship hadn't meant a thing last night. I had fucked up big-time.

I was in the shower for over an hour, and I could tell because the water started to run cold. I stepped out of the shower quietly, then tried to ease my way into the living room without waking Rene. I knew she would be up any minute, once she realized I was no longer next to her. I crept back into the bedroom after I was fully clothed and climbed back on my side of the bed. Only seconds after my head hit the pillow, I fell into a deep sleep.

Jasmine was talking to me, and in walked Peaches, appearing out of nowhere. I couldn't catch a break, and James' bedroom was the last place I needed to be spotted with two chicks. "I'm not interrupting anything, am I?" Peaches asked. Her smile was real crooked, and I was almost glad she had walked in so Jasmine could get off my jock.

I hoped that Peaches's entrance would start Jasmine on a whole new subject or, better yet, downplay her freaky groove. She had gone on and on about how she was digging me and wanted to be down with me. She had even gone as far as to say that she didn't give a damn if I had a girl. Now, I wasn't new to the game, but I surely was new to the scene. I thought I had misunderstood her when she insisted on being with me, knowing that I had a woman at home. I tried to shake her, but those damn lips and that smile melted me all over again. She scooted closer and closer to me, trying to squeeze her way into my space. I rubbed my chin and watched her closely. She started removing her clothes like there wasn't nothing to it but to do it. First went her net and then the short dress she had on underneath. I watched her remove her panties and bra, and she did this without minding that Peaches was nearby, in the restroom, and capable of walking in. I smiled, shaking my head, trying to prematurely withdraw myself from what was about to go down.

"Come on, Mama," I told her. We both had had one too many drinks. The liquor was talking to me, and I could tell that the Hpnotiq had already spoken to her. She forced me back onto the bed. She began slow dancing and shaking her ass in front of me, as the music could still be heard through the walls. She flipped the light switch, dimmed the lights a little bit more than they had been, and climbed on top of me. Her legs straddled me loosely, and she was ass naked. She pressed her perky titties in my face and forced me to enjoy it. I tried not to, but the drink was still doing its thang. I placed the empty glass on the nightstand and watched her like a thief in the night.

Even though it was dark as hell, I could still see her from the light that crept from underneath the bathroom door. All of a sudden that light vanished. I lay back, still trying to talk Jasmine up off me, but the fight in me had left. I was too weak and vulnerable. Wanting but not wanting. Needing some pussy but not being able to get to it. She slid her hands up and down my body, positioned my hands onto her soft, round ass. She wanted me to feel every thrusting movement she made. I tried to sit up. She pushed me back, forcing me to lie down, and suddenly climbed onto my face and glided herself down easily and steadily. Next, I felt pubic hairs tickling my chin and riding my face.

This isn't Rene, I kept reminding myself. I forced my head back and tried to turn away, telling her, "We can't do this."

"Uh-uh, baby. I want you. I need you. I saw how you were looking at me. I know you want this. James paid for this pussy for you to enjoy tonight, so I'm delivering it."

I finally caught the voice, and it was no longer Jasmine who was on top of me, but it was Peaches. She fucked and rode my face like a pro. The next thing I knew, she tried to go down on me, but I refused. When she saw how quickly I jumped the hell up, she knew what time it was. Figuring I had never been touched down there, she avoided the area. I looked to my right, because I could feel another body lying there. It was Jasmine. I could tell by that sweet vanilla scent that had been on her body all night. She was lying next to me, holding my right hand and finger fucking herself with her other hand. These women were as wild as they came.

I better get my ass up out of here while I still can. I tried to help myself by easing up, but Peaches was on my leg once again, trying to spread her pussy juices. She had also removed all her clothing and was humping me like a dog in heat.

"Come on. Take your clothes off," they both kept saying.

I knew if I did that, things would only get worse. Jasmine was still at my side, pulling at my boxers, playing with her nipples. Peaches was in between Jasmine's legs, getting her grub on, allowing me the pleasure of watching. Jasmine moaned in pleasure and pulled and dug her nails into my arms with every movement that Peaches made. She had to be going to work down there, because I was certain that Jasmine had my damn arm bleeding. I was ready for her to reach her orgasm so I could get the fuck up and be gone.

Just as the thought entered my mind, Peaches said, "Now, this is not right. Jazzy. We are having too much fun, and Sand here ain't participatin'. How rude of us."

"No, no." I shook my head. "I'm enjoying myself, really, so you girls go right on ahead and keep doin' what you doin'."

Before I could say any more, Peaches had her long tongue halfway down my throat, compelling me to surrender to her. I sampled a little bit of what Jasmine tasted like from Peaches's tongue. She was sweet and tasty. Almost too tasty. Jasmine had lifted up my undershirt and had exposed my underdeveloped breasts. She began sucking them, making them grow erect. I tried to fight every feeling that both of them were anxious to let out. I could no longer hold back. I moved Peaches to the side and climbed on top of Jasmine and fucked the shit out of her. I ran my fingers in her so deep, I could have sworn my arm was almost fully in. She was wet as hell, deep like an ocean, pouring like a waterfall, and that was the way I liked it. She turned me on more than Peaches, and I wanted so badly to dine inside of her.

I kept telling myself that I didn't know her and had no idea if she was involved with someone or not. I didn't like to invade OPP—other people's pussy—and I damn sure did not want to bring anything back to Rene. I was dead serious about that. I knew from the jump that if I engaged myself any further, I was putting myself at risk.

Fuck it. I was hot, and this girl was about to get a piece of something she had never had. After I made her climax with my fingers for the second time, while "So Beautiful," by Joe, played in the background, I decided to do some shit she probably ain't never had done in her entire life.

"Get on top of me and ride my face," I demanded.

She did as she was told, and Peaches watched from the sidelines, trying to get in anywhere she fit in every chance she got. I sucked on Jasmine's pussy until she was mumbling through clenched teeth. She grabbed my braids to hang on to while I took her for a horseback ride. And the moment I realized her steamy juices were about to boil over, I inserted my index finger in her tight asshole and fondled her tits with my other hand, all while chastising her pussy, as if it were mine and mine only.

The only sounds that were escaping Jasmine's mouth were, "Ooh, damn. Daddy, don't stop. Please, Sand, don't quit."

Soon after that, the spell was cast. Drips of what she had left in her came rushing out and into my mouth. She tasted sweet, like a red apple slice dipped in warm, sticky caramel. When we were finished, and once I saw that the sun was coming up, I left and dashed home, ready to get my ass chewed out.

I woke up to Rene standing over me as I lay in bed. "What time did you get home?" Her arms were folded, and I could tell she wasn't trying to hear shit but the truth. I wanted to lie, but I didn't know how far that would get me, so I told the semi truth.

"I got home at three, babe. You were asleep, so I didn't want to wake you. Me and the guys stayed up playing dominoes and drinking." I knew I was lying through my teeth, but she didn't.

To make my story stick, I grabbed my wallet off the dresser and counted out twelve hundred dollars. Six of that I had won, four hundred I had collected from the peeps as a graduation gift, and the other two hundred I had already had.

She believed me and rushed over to double count the money herself. "Damn, baby.You are good," she said, all excited. "I'm gonna have to sign you up in some local tournaments."

"Nah. They have too many rules. They wouldn't be able to hang with me, anyway," I bragged. She laughed and asked me how much of that money was her allowance. I looked at her crazily.

"Here. Take all of it. You know I don't have you on a damn allowance. When I got it, you got it. Understand? Put some of it in the bank, though." I knew Rene knew how to save and put a little back for rainy days, so I wasn't trippin'. I kept a bill fifty and handed her the rest.

I went on with my day like it was any other day. I got on the Internet and checked out some buildings that were going to be rented out and some that were going to be sold. I needed a building large enough to put a runway stage through and to hold a nice-sized crowd. I ran across a building for sale, and it said the seller was willing to negotiate and was motivated to sell. They wanted forty thousand dollars for the building. I wrote down the information and kept browsing. I knew that building was what I was looking for when I couldn't find a better deal.

I met up with Timothy McChester the following evening. He was the real estate agent assigned to the property. He walked me around the large former warehouse, pointing to spots that could be easily altered.

"Believe it or not, the previous owner had turned this into a nightclub," Timothy said.

I rubbed my chin, feeling out the idea of a twenty-thousand-something-odd-square-foot warehouse being a club. He told me the club used to be called Blue Jays. He said it had been a young hip-hop club, but it hadn't lasted six months.

See, I knew that hip-hop clubs in Dallas were always opening. Everyone wanted a damn club. I had bigger and better plans, which were gon' clock in major dough. Just as I was imagining the spotlights and the glamorous settings, Timothy intervened, interrupting my thoughts.

"So what are you planning to use this building for?"

I stared up at the tall ceiling and said, "I plan on bringing New York to Dallas."

"What?" He looked at me, confused and dumbfounded.

"I plan on turning this building into one of Dallas's first and largest club talent search agencies. I plan to have the city's finest talent come to life right here in this building. I'm going to have models, rappers, singers, dancers, and the whole nine right here in this building. It's time our talent became exposed."

He was now looking at me as if the idea suddenly seemed real. I had to admit that I had learned a lot while living on the streets. I knew that life was hard knocks, and I wanted to give some of those people out there a chance to make their dreams come true. There were just too many uneducated people on the street—too many potential lawyers, doctors, police officers, rappers, singers—who had talent. God-given gifts they didn't know what to do with. I wanted to expose them, help them help themselves. I knew Timothy was feeling me. He told me that I could probably get a grant easily. I was already ahead of him by ten steps. My next thought was where I would put that runway.

When I got home, Rene was not there. She had left early that morning. The sun had gone down, and night had fallen. I couldn't believe she had been gone all day without calling me to check in and let me know she was okay. She knew that I didn't like her out after dark unless I knew where she was and who she was with. I started getting worried.

I looked out front, and her car was still not there. Not knowing where she could be made me even more upset. I called her cell several times, only to be greeted by the damn voice mail. When I didn't get an answer, I slipped on my house shoes and started toward the front door. I roamed around the damn apartment complex until my feet were sore. I didn't know if walking around, looking for her, made me think I would find her any sooner or what. I guessed I was hoping to find her at our little Laundromat, washing some clothes or something. I checked there, but the door was locked. Where was she at this time of night? I was pissed off and past worried because Rene had her nerve to pull some shit like this.

I walked back toward the apartment. As I turned the key in the door, she was opening it.

"Where the hell you been?" I yelled, slamming the door behind me. She almost jumped out of her skin.

"Just doing my run, baby. I didn't get to do it earlier, because it was so hot out." She looked at me like I was crazy for asking such a thing, but at that moment, I didn't care what the fuck she thought. Her eyes were locked on mine, and I had no reason not to believe her. She had no reason to lie to me. Besides, people did run at the track across the street late at night.

I removed my shirt, leaving on my sports bra, and totally missed the arm of the couch when I was trying to hang it there. That was when I thought I was seeing things. My eyes had to be playing tricks on me. Rene turned around to face me.

Walking closer to her, trying to get a better view of what my eyes were focused on, I said, "I know like all hell that ain't no muthafuckin' hickey on your neck."

Her face went numb, and her body froze like a statue.

Sand

She grabbed at her neck, trying to locate the incredibly huge red mark my eyes were pointing to. I felt my veins starting to pop out and my muscles contracting and tightening. I was waiting for her to tell me why the fuck there was a mark as bright as day on the right side of her neck.

"Baby, this ain't no hickey!" she exclaimed, looking into the compact mirror she had retrieved from her purse. "A mosquito bit me earlier." She looked straight into my eyes. My emotions were starting to come down, but I had to catch myself. My woman was staring into my eyes, telling me that what I was seeing was not what I was seeing. She placed the mirror on the kitchen bar and brushed her soft fingers down my forehead and my nose, halting at my lips. "Babe, how could you think such a thing?"

I released a sigh while visually inspecting her all over. I wasn't falling for that shit. I snatched off her shirt, her jeans, her bra, and then off went her panties. I searched over her entire body, trying to find any mark or scar that had not been there before she walked out that door. After laying her down on our love seat and examining every area of her body as if I were her gynecologist, I came to the conclusion that it was evidently a mosquito bite. I was relieved, and my guard went back down.

"Damn, baby, I thought you were goin' to slap me for a moment there."

I stared back into her eyes, stroked her chin ever so lightly, and said, "I was."

She must have not taken me seriously, because she brushed me off. She got up and walked around the house, ass naked, picking up small pieces of scattered paper I had left on the floor. Rene was a neat freak and always made sure the house was spick-and-span. You would have thought she cleaned houses for a living. That was another quality she had that had attracted me to her—her cleanliness when it came to her home and her body. I watched her clean and dust until watching her roam free, naked like that, became too unbearable.

"Come here, Rene," I said.

She walked toward me, fiddling with her hair.

"You know I love you, right?" In my mind, we were about to have makeup sex for all the things that I would have done to her had she not explained herself. I had envisioned grabbing her by her neck and squeezing it until she came clean with me. I had seen all my inside rage and anger building up, and it would have made me do things to her I would not have wanted to do. I loved Rene, and the thought of her hurting me intentionally was hard to take. I knew she would never do anything like that to me. Rene was mine, and I could never see her with anyone else. Those had images faded, and I had felt real bad afterward for even letting such a thing trip me up so bad.

I picked her up, laid her back on the sofa, and tossed her salad right there. Moans of pleasure filled the living room immediately, but that was only the foreplay action. I carried her into our bedroom, all while imagining how I was about to rip some shit up. I rolled my lips over her breasts so gently. I tickled and teased each nipple with the tip of my moist tongue, creating a creamy, sticky glaze, indicating where my mouth had been seconds earlier. Her areolae seemed as if they grew darker and darker from the touch. Her eyes remained closed, and all that she was mumbling went unheard as I feasted below for yet another round.

I felt like a little kid in a candy store, exploring all the sweets, sampling all the free goodies. Her Kit Kat tasted like chocolate-covered strawberries that had been marinated in wine, and the insides of her thighs were like a sweet-tasting butterscotch candy cane. I stimulated her clit with the hardness of my tongue and watched her squirm vigorously while digging her nails into my flesh. I then removed my shorts and let my boxers fall free to the floor. I inched one finger and then two fingers inside her love, slowly preparing her for my grand entrance. I savored her sweet love juices left behind on my fingers, sucking both of them dry.

Just when I got the clue that she was wanting and ready, I grabbed my handy black strap-on from underneath the mattress and made love to her like there was no tomorrow. I hit that G-spot, fondled her clit, and sucked her sweet coated Almond Joys. Her soft moans turned into strong demands.

"Sand, fuck me harder," she yelled. And so I did.

She grabbed my ass and gripped it as her body rocked with each thrust I made. She sucked on my chin and bit down slightly on my lips, arousing me even more. I got off on her loud moans and screams of pleasure.

I did that shit. I made that happen. She climaxed twice, back-to-back, but I was going for number three.

The bright morning sun stung my face and neck. I reached over, and Rene was not beside me. I sat up quickly, trying to remember if she had woken me to tell me she was leaving to go somewhere. But then I spotted a quickly scribbled note lying on the nightstand.

Baby, I'm at Shun's house. Call me when you wake up. Love ya, Rene.

The alarm clock read 10:15 a.m. It was a bright Sunday morning, and normally Rene went with her best friend, Shun, to church.

Shun was crazy and had a habit of getting into everyone's business. If there was any type of situation or problem, the wannabe life coach was at your service. She was all ears when it came to drama and gossip. The "gossip to go, expedited delivery" queen always made sure she had an earful to dish back out to somebody else.

I had never trusted or liked her, and there was no telling what rumors she had about Rene and me floating around the church among her gossip clique. Whenever she came around, she always questioned Rene about our sex life, asking about her happiness with her chosen lifestyle. Who in the hell had appointed her to play God? She always had something to say about everything. Now, I wasn't gonna be the one to tell sister girl that she had no room in hell to talk. But I wished somebody would. I tried to spare her feelings, but she was pushing it.

Truth be told, she sat over there in a two-bedroom apartment with four kids, all by different daddies, and no husband or sign of a man. She had no job, low self-esteem, and she dressed like an old-ass woman who shopped at the neighborhood thrift store. She stayed in and out of other people's lives because she was too unhappy with her own. And with all the drama and shit she continued to stir up, she had the nerve to claim she was saved and sanctified. She had told me and Rene that she was a changed woman and she walked a straight line. Like hell she was.

What really had me upset was when she started getting in Rene's ear and all up in our sex life.

"How you gonna know how a man feel if you ain't never been with one?" she had asked Rene. And she had damn near killed me when she tried to quote scriptures from the Bible. She had tried to make Rene believe that all lesbians made it their mission to convert heterosexual women. I had even tried explaining to Shun that I was born gay. She had had the nerve to tell me that I was the Antichrist. After that, I hadn't even bothered trying to explain. Just like everyone else, she was going to believe what she wanted to believe.

I didn't understand how Rene could even remain friends with her ignorant, insensitive, and clueless ass. She acted as though I had on some sort of costume that could be put on and taken off. I had heard plenty of stories of how women became gay or got turned out, but not me. I wasn't abused or molested as a child. I had always loved women, and for me, it was a natural thing.

I hated to do it, but after I read Rene's note, I called Shun's house to talk to Rene. Before being able to speak to my girl, I had to hear Shun's shit.

"So will you be joining us in church today, Cassandra?"

My jaw tightened at the mention of my full name. Why in the hell did Rene have to share that personal information with her?

"Not today, Shun," I said as pleasantly as I could. "But you ladies have a good time."

"Oh, we always have a good time listening to the Word from the Lord. Maybe you should join us and see how soon you turn around and see the light."

I pulled the phone away from my ear a little because this smart-ass was already getting on my nerves. I could detect the sarcasm in her rude ass. I heard her scream out to one of the kids, telling them to tell their aunt that Cassandra was on the phone.

"Don't worry, Cassandra, I will personally pray for you."

Rene finally came to the phone.

"Hey, hon," I said, relieved that Looney Tunes was off the phone.

"Hey, babe. So you're finally up?"

"Yeah, but I'm missing you."

"I miss you too, Sand, but I really miss that little escapade we had going on last night."

I smiled, also remembering. How could I forget? She had achieved a new record, cumming back-to-back that many times. "Um, wanna go for round four tonight?" I teased, referring to how many times she'd climaxed in an hour.

The thought was interrupted when I saw a familiar number light up on my cell as it vibrated.

"Baby, let me catch this call coming through," I told her, watching the caller ID display of my cell phone.

"All right, baby. I'll see you when church is over."

"All right. Love you," I said quickly. Then I clicked off one phone and hit TALK on the other.

"Jasmine, I thought I told you not to call me like this!" I exclaimed.

There was nothing but silence on the other end of the phone. I walked through the house, trying to determine if my cell had faded out or if she had hung up after I'd answered. I looked at the display, and my screen saver of me and Rene was on the screen. I started to redial her number. I was sure it was Jasmine who had called because of the area code. I was over here in the 214 part of town, and she was in the 817 side of town.

After that night at James's house, she had practically begged me for my cell phone number. I had given it to her but had told her it was just as friends, sensing that she wanted it to be more than that. I had called her the very next morning, trying to clear up things about the previous night.

"I just don't want you to jump to any conclusions," I had explained. "I love my girl, and I'm not leaving her."

She had promised me that our little fling would remain where we had left it, back at the condo and in the guest room. We had chatted a few more times that day, exchanging small talk but nothing serious. Then, out of the blue, she had blurted out that she wasn't new to this. Before I could say anything, she had gone on to share with me things I wished she had never brought up, as she had tried to convince me she was no virgin to the lifestyle. I had tried to play innocent. I had had nothing to say. I had just listened and played the role of a friend.

"Sand, I've been involved with women for over a year now, so don't think you turned me out."

I stopped whatever the hell I was doing and immediately shot back, "Baby girl, I am the last one to try to turn you out. That's not my job. I'll leave that to the others. The ones that would be more than happy to make you their little play toy, or shall I say, experiment."

"What the hell you mean by that?"

"Look, Jasmine, it wasn't a secret that I'm gay. I mean, look at me. So I already figured you were cuttin' strong when you slipped me your number, remember?" She was silent, but I kept talking, luring her into my world for a second. "So if you have the slightest idea running through your head that I was intending on turning you out, you can erase it. I am already involved with someone. Turning you out is not gon' benefit me any."

She was still quiet. She must have had her head on twisted if she thought I was out to flip her around. Even though I could sense that she was inexperienced and had never been with a woman before that night at James's crib, the day we fucked, I left it at that. Her trying to turn the shit around, opposed to coming straight out and being honest, had sparked a red flag with me. I mean, who was she trying to impress? She wasn't dealing with a rookie, and I damn sure wasn't no amateur. If an animal could distinguish their kind, what made her think I couldn't? Family knew family. Some females were more curious than a muthafucka but just never had the guts or the boldness to say it. They would beat around the bush and say shit like "I ain't never did it, but I know it ain't for me," or "I tried it, but we were just playing around." When you heard that *but*, then you knew you were dealing with a confused or rather clueless chick.

My years in high school had taught me how to distinguish the G crowds and the B crowds, and then you had the BC crowds. That was the gay, the bisexual, and the bi-curious. As they said, birds of a feather flocked together. And one thing was for sure: women talked. So if they had a best friend or a homegirl who was down with family, nine times out of ten, they tried it and denied it, or they claimed it and then shamed it. In other words, they became down-low freaks who got busy when they felt like it, under their own terms and rules. The ones who weren't bold enough to just come out and say they did women or were curious to know how it felt to be with one were the down-low sistas who like to be fucked and teased by a man but licked and pleased by a woman.

It was more of a mental thing with those kinds. Being free to tap into both worlds anytime they damn well pleased. Those kinds wanted to have their cake and eat it too. I couldn't explain it. I just knew they existed, and if you a man, you had better not leave your girl around. You grabbed her arms and gripped your balls, pulling her close to you, when you saw a nigga like me checking her out. But Sand wasn't the one you needed to be worried about. It was the girl's best friend,

Regina, the one whose house she slept at when hubby was out of town.

My brain was throbbing, but I managed to keep talking. "So, do you know Peaches?" I asked, switching the subject a tad bit.

"Yeah, I know her. She works for Chyna."

"Chyna?" I was shocked.

"Yeah, she one of Chyna's girls. She's been down with her for a minute."

I shook my head, because I had had no idea. I was sure as hell that I was busted out now. I just knew that it was only a matter of time before that shit would get back to Rene.

Returning to the present moment, I decided against calling Jasmine back, figuring that if it was something important, she would call me back. She never did, and that was a good thing.

I got to work. Time flew by while I was working. I had placed ads a few weeks ago in several of the local nightlife publications and chat-room boards online. I had even had radio play. The response had been overwhelming. Men and women from all over the metroplex were trying to get down. Models of all sizes and ethnic backgrounds had sent in snapshots. Rappers and other singers had sent in demo tapes, and comedians and crowd pleasers had sent in videos. On this day I was able to get through only a few at a time, putting my okay picks in a pile for Rene to check out later.

It was one o' clock, and she was probably on her way home from church. I wanted to surprise her when she arrived by ordering some takeout from Sweet Georgia Brown, but the idea vanished when I heard loud footsteps and kids running up the stairs. I knew then that we had guests, and if it was who I thought it was, then off to the bedroom I was about to go.

Rene walked in, looking stunning, as always. She was rocking a lavender dress with silver trim around the edges. It stopped right above her knees. Her long hair was pulled back into a tight bun, and her makeup was flawless, matching her outfit. She had on clear sandals, and her toes sported a fresh pedicure with French tips. I wanted to run over and sop her up like some hot water corn bread with collard greens and sweet tea, but I had to maintain my composure. She walked over and gave me a hug, trying not to put on a show in front of Shun's kids, who had come into the house right behind her. I spoke to all four of them, and just when I was about to shut the front door, in walked the devil herself, Miss Shun—all 290 pounds of her in a bright Kool-Aid red outfit. She ignored me, walked past me, and sat her happy ass down on the sofa.

"Hello, Miss Shun," I said. She had her nerve to walk up in my house, right past me, and not speak. I paid the damn bills.

"Hi, Cassandra." She hated to have to be face-to-face with me, but frankly, I didn't give a damn. She was in my spot.

I walked over to Rene. "Baby, I'm gon' be in the room." She could tell I was displeased with her friend's rudeness, but I was not about to let Shun's silly circus ass ruin my Sunday afternoon. Without another word, I walked into my room and left them to tend to their own business.

Rene

My life had always been difficult. It had been so when I was younger, growing up in the foster care system, and it was now. My girlfriend, Sand, who liked for me to refer to her as my man or my boyfriend, was old news. I mean, I still loved her, but I was tired of living a sheltered life. Life was just cruel to people like us, and I was just tired. I couldn't keep living this way. Hoping and praying that when I walk out my door, I wouldn't be a victim of some horrible hate crime or be laughed at and teased because of the life I represented.

I was walking out of the grocery store, nervously watching the two young black guys following behind. Seeing that I had only one bag, I knew they weren't offering to help me. They began shouting for me to come back so they could check out my ass. I got in my car, still ignoring their asses, letting their tired game fall on deaf ears.

"Come on, li'l mama. If you got a man, all you gotta do is say so. I ain't mad at ya. But then again, fuck that nigga! He ain't no friend of mines. That means we can still bump and grind," one of them yelled.

This wannabe-ass Romeo. Who the hell did he think he was? I looked back at him and his boy, smiled at the one trying to play mack daddy. They were both jacked the fuck up. One had his pants hanging halfway off his ass, and the other . . . well, there was just no hope at all for him. He was the main one skinnin' and grinnin' with them gapped teeth and oversize lips. The only thing that I could say was cute about him was the fact that he was so ugly but still made an effort to impress a woman by wearing some strong-ass cologne that put a stinging on your nose when you passed by. Probably a homemade blend of Mama and Daddy's last Christmas perfume and cologne sets.

Little Romeo had on some blue jean pants with a long white T-shirt that damn near hung down to his knees, and from the looks of it, he had another one on underneath it, even though it was every bit a hundred degrees outside. And what was that in his mouth? Oh, Lord, I thought clip-ons were out of style. Were they still sporting the clip-on teeth? I wondered. I had to suppress my laugh. I started my car and turned the air conditioner on full blast. I was in a hurry and had no time to converse with the little wannabes. I was on a mission. I had to do what I had to do and still try to beat Sand home before she started trippin' out.

"Come on, Mama, with your fine ass. Give a nigga with pay the time of day so I can play." Little Romeo pulled out a wad of bills that were rolled up tightly beneath a brown rubber band. For a moment I wanted to go over there and show him what a real stack of bills looked like, but I realized that under that twenty, he, like other young boys I had come in contact with, probably had a bundle of one-dollar bills.

Talk about highsiding and straight fronting. The numbers inside my checkbook register that reflected my last deposit and my account balance would make his little chunky ass feel broker than a two-dollar ho. But because I knew how to be sweet, I didn't want to embarrass the little off-brand shoes—wearing wanksta. I put my car in drive.

"Fuck you, then, you conceited-ass ho. Shit, you must be crazy to turn down a nigga like me. I'm a muthafuckin' playa! Ya heard me! Shit, I can pimp mo' hoes that's way finer than you. Prissy-ass biatch!" He turned to his boy. "Come on, my nigga. Let's leave that stuck-up ho alone."

"Man, I bet that bitch gay. Ole dykin' ass!" his boy said. They laughed.

I stepped on my brakes so fast that my purse in the backseat flew up to the front. I rolled down my window enough to stick my left hand out and waved the middle finger proudly.

And that was why a decent woman would never give them the time of day, I assured myself. That was the problem with some of these young men. They didn't know how to talk to a lady, and when they did, it eventually became an invitation to a fuck party or a one-night stand. I would respect a man more if he just came out with it and said what he wanted. It was hard to find a man who had a job, his own ride, and, most importantly, his own spot. Those three qualifications that some of us women looked for were hard to come by in a man. Even though I wasn't out searching for dick, I still had my preferences. I knew some women who settled for the first Dick or Harry who paid them any attention at all. He could have no job and still be living at home with his mama. As long as he had a big swagger and the woman's kids could call him Daddy, shit, he was in the door.

I bumped my Destiny's Child CD and hummed to the beat of "Soldier," trying to calm my nerves.

I need a soldier. . . . Where they at, where they at. . . .

My cell phone was ringing, and I knew who it was by the ringtone. Sand was probably back at home by now and wondering where the hell I could be at this time of night by myself. I had left the house right behind her, giving her at least a twenty-minute head start. She kept blowing up my cell phone. Every time I looked down, there was an incoming call from home, but I had some serious business I needed to handle that excluded her.

I finally made it back to the house. I pulled up into the driveway, announcing my arrival with the garage-door opener. I opened my glove compartment, slipped my cold ice onto my left ring finger, and got out of my car, carrying the Wal-Mart bag and my key to the beautiful three-bedroom, twenty-five-hundred-square-foot house. I walked inside, entering through the kitchen.

"Vincent, Vincent," I yelled. "I'm back, baby."

He came from the computer room, shut the door behind him, and headed toward me. He reached for the bag, then pulled out the box that was inside. I watched him as he tore it open, as if the answer would already be there. When he realized how much I was shaking, he grabbed my trembling hands, and that gave me immediate reassurance. I felt a tear slide down my left cheek, and he wiped it gently away with his right thumb. We walked slowly toward the hallway bathroom. He stopped me before I could go in.

"Rene, no matter what this test says, I still want to marry you. I just wanted you to know that." He paused. "No matter what, I'm here."

I noticed a couple of tears also beginning to form in his big blue eyes. We both stood there, hoping to find comfort in each other. There was a brief silence. My emotions were so scattered that I didn't know what to do. Did I want a positive result, or did I want a negative one? The two outcomes bounced back and forth in my head as I mentally prepared myself for either.

I let go of Vincent's hands and walked into the bathroom, then shut the door behind me. I began reading the small text on the box, line by line. I followed the instructions, careful not to make a mistake. To ensure that I got an accurate result, I urinated in the Styrofoam cup and dipped the end of the stick in it.

In sixty seconds my life could change drastically. I turned my back and slowly counted from one to ten. *Oh God. Oh God.* When I turned back around to face the counter, where I had laid down my test, I was caught off guard by the pink plus sign. I quickly grabbed the test stick to take a closer look at the results. My eyes almost jumped out of their sockets when the pink plus sign grew darker and darker as the seconds passed. I snatched the leaflet from the box the test had come in, then went over every step in detail. The test stick had definitely given me a positive result. The hands that were shaking uncontrollably before were now covering my mouth in astonishment and rubbing my belly. I smiled. There was an instant love that I had for this child growing inside of me.

"Rene, is everything all right in there?"

I unlocked the door, and Vincent walked in cautiously, looking nervous and scared all at once. I couldn't talk. Not only was I at a loss for words, but my heart was also beating extra fast. Vincent came to witness the same thing I had.

"Does... does this mean we're pregnant?" Tears began streaming down my face like they had earlier.

Vincent had the biggest smile spread across his face than I had ever seen in our thirteen months of dating. He was happier now than he had been when I accepted his proposal of marriage. I remembered that day like it was yesterday.

On that day Vincent had taken me to Ramiliano's, a fancy, expensive Italian restaurant on the rich folks' side of town. He had told me to get all dressed up because he was taking me to meet some important friends of his who were hosting a party.

I had had to lie to Sand real good and tell her that I had been invited to one of Shun's brothers' social gatherings. I knew that when she heard Shun's name, it made her sick to her stomach, so I wasn't worried about her asking to join me.

I wore a beautiful black evening gown, a silver choker, and earrings that dangled almost to my shoulders, and I carried a three-hundred-dollar handbag, which I clutched tightly to my side. My thick jet-black hair flowed down my back and across my shoulder blades. My makeup was done to perfection with a hint of MAC Lipglass shining over my chocolate-kiss lipstick. I had to admit, I was dazzling from head to toe.

Vincent had not given me any details about how the evening was scheduled to go. He had said only that I should act natural and just be myself. Once we reached the exotic restaurant, I was overwhelmed. The scenery was beautiful. I swore I had never seen anything like it before. It was very upscale. Sand could never afford to take me to a place like this, and even if she could, she wouldn't have the time.

I admired everything about the place before I even stepped foot through the doors. Beautiful golden lights were shining on the patrons who were outside, dining in the breezy night air, as waiters and waitresses escorted others to their seats, then placed their cloth napkins in their laps for them. A live band entertained the crowd. As soon as we walked in, we were seated at a table that seemed to have been sectioned off from the rest of the crowd intentionally. I figured that they were out of seats, so they had had no choice but to sit us there, considering that the place was so crowded with people who were dining and having drinks.

I was glad to have selected my black dress, given the attire that everyone else wore. All the ladies in the place looked to be in their midthirties or older. If I were to guess, Vincent and I were probably the youngest couple in the building. Vincent was twenty-seven, and I had a couple more months before I made twenty-one.

I smiled, admiring Vincent as I reflected on when we had met.

"Rene, I got somebody that wanna meet you at this bank where I opened my child support account at," Shun said.

"Who wants to meet me at a bank?"

"You'll see. He's expecting to meet you today. Just get ready. I'm on my way."

Later we pulled up into the bank's parking lot. Once inside, Shun walked me over to his desk.

"Vincent, this is my best friend, Rene, who I've been telling you about."

He stood up from his seat and reached out for my hand. He shook it and then came around to pull out a chair for me. "How are you doing, ma'am? I'm Vincent Montgomery. Your friend has told me so much about you, I feel like I know you already."

I smiled, knowing he probably did feel like he knew me if Shun was doing the talking.

"Now can I get my free gift?" I heard Shun ask him. She walked over to the bank's display of blenders and grabbed the one right on the top.

"That damn girl," I whispered.

"He's too old, Shun," I told her later.

"Girl, no he not. He's just the right age. Maybe he can teach you a thing or two, if you know what I mean. Well, then again, you know what they say about those white men. Let me know if it's true."

"*Shun, I am not about to sleep with that man. Damn. We just met. Not only that, I'm with someone. You know Sand would kill me if she even thought I was feeling out another guy. A white boy at that.*"

"*Chile, please. Sand ain't rockin' what he rockin' or packin' what he aint lackin'. Ha-ha.*"

"*Shun, you gon' get me killed, I swear. You and your bright ideas.*"

"*You'll thank me later, honey. Trust that.*"

Ever since then, Vincent and I had been an item.

The waitress came over to our table with medium-size crystal glasses of water and warm white cloth napkins. I ordered the special of the night, and Vincent ordered some type of pasta entrée that he said the place was famous for. After we ate and talked a little about life and the things we both wanted out of it, Vincent waved to our server so that she would remove our plates. She smiled at me at least a hundred times before she made a secretive gesture at Vincent.

No more than a minute later, the band, which had been playing soft music, completely stopped, and the band members redirected their attention to the middle of the room, where we were sitting. I looked up to the second floor and saw crowds of people standing there, staring down at us, and those that I had seen outside earlier had now moved indoors. I was now looking all over the place, trying to figure out what was going on and why the music had stopped suddenly. The spotlight used for the band was now shining on me and Vincent. When I looked back up at Vincent, he had already positioned himself on the rug that was underneath our table, with one knee pointing down to the floor and the other facing ahead. He held a shiny silver ring, which I knew had to be platinum. It encased a large, beautiful oval-shaped diamond. I could not believe what I was seeing, and I damn sure couldn't believe the size of that ring. I tried my best to hold back the tears that were starting to fall, but I failed. Vincent was now staring into my eyes, and I was staring into his. I had hoped for this moment to come, but I hadn't expected it to come so soon.

"Rene, I love you. You are the best thing that has ever happened to me. You are the most beautiful woman I have ever laid eyes on. Your touch, your smile, everything about you, I admire. I would be the happiest man in the world right now if you promised me that I could wake up to your beautiful face every day of the week."

I felt my heart skip a beat, and my bladder was calling for attention. Butterflies were floating in my stomach, and chill bumps had broken out. I just knew I was about to faint.

"Please, Rene, make me that happy man today." He was now reaching for my left hand and still holding the ring in his right. "Rene, will you marry me?"

Everything became a blur. The tears that had welled in my eyes began streaming down my face, causing my mascara to run and my eyes to burn. Any problem that I had had before I walked through those double green doors had disappeared. He and about two hundred other people waited for my response. I was still trying to get a grip and catch my breath. The words that formed in my throat seemed to be stuck, leaving me speechless. After some motivation from the crowd, I was able to bring myself to utter a few words.

"Yes . . . yes, Vincent, I would be honored to be your wife. I will marry you."

Everyone started clapping and yelling. Glasses were held up in the air, and so were bottles of expensive champagne. People were making toasts to us from afar. The spotlight had moved from our table to the dance floor, and everyone was cheering us on. Vincent and I stood up, and he guided me to the center of the floor. I remembered us dancing the night away, enjoying life, enjoying us.

Now Vincent watched as the pink plus sign on the test stick grew clearer. He was in shock as much as I was.

"When did we have time to make this baby?" he blurted out. "We hardly ever see each other." He was smiling, all the while holding the end of the test stick. It was odd, but I was wondering the exact same thing. He started rubbing on my belly and massaging my back, enjoying the fact that he was about to be a father. Finally, I had an explanation for why I hadn't had a period for two months.

Vincent took me by the hand, led me out of the bathroom and back into the living room. He removed my shoes, my jeans, and then started for my shirt. I lay down on the sofa, in disbelief, too exhausted to leave right away.

"Rene, talk to me, baby. What are you thinking about?"

It was clear that my mind had completely drifted off to some other place.

"Rene, I know this isn't perfect timing, with our living situation and all, but we can work this out. I say we move the wedding date up."

I looked at him like he had lost his mind. For one, I didn't recall setting a date yet, and two, *we* couldn't work shit out. I was not about to have this baby like this. I mean, I didn't believe in abortions, but I was not quite ready for a child. We hadn't had a chance to enjoy us yet. We were still young. We weren't even officially married. He wanted to move the wedding date up, but I was in no rush. I wanted us to take our time getting to know each other a little more, even if that meant a long engagement. We hardly knew anything about each other. It was already bad that we had to see each other when my timing was convenient. And when I said our time together was limited, I was talking one day out of the week.

I could never call him from my home. That would get me busted for real. I hadn't even volunteered my home phone number and prayed he wouldn't ask for anything more than the cell number I had given him. Sand wasn't having that shit. No way, nohow. She would be right to suspect something if a man had the nerve to call our house, where she paid all the bills, asking if they could talk to her woman. If you weren't a bill collector or someone she knew, then you could hang it up. Even though she swore men didn't intimidate her, I felt like deep inside they did. They possessed something she would never have. And when it was all said and done, she still bled out the pussy once a month, just like I did.

Vincent began caressing parts of my body that he knew would become aroused. I tried to fight it, but there was no use. He sucked on my neck and kissed me from head to toe. He slid his hand in my panties. I grabbed it, moved it back to his side.

"What's wrong, Rene?" He was looking at me as if I had no say in what he was doing and as if he was mad that I had stopped him.

"I need to be going," I said firmly. He had already got me in this predicament, and now I had to hurry home to sort this shit out.

"I know you have a sick grandma and all, but can't you get somebody else to take care of her tonight?"

I looked at him and said no. I was one hell of an actor. I hated lying to him, but I had to—to save my ass and probably his too. I had him believing that I had a sick elderly grandmother who was suffering from Alzheimer's and could remember only me. He thought that I took care of her every day of the week and that this was the reason why we were able to see each other only when it was suitable for me. I couldn't bring myself to tell him the truth—that his loving soon-to-be wife was a well-known dyke on the other side of town, whose girlfriend was a popular butch. He would probably spaz the fuck out. Vincent was clearly homophobic. I had seen how he would look at the openly gay men who ate lunch together at some of the restaurants we would go to on his lunch break. "Come on. Let's leave, Rene. Too many fags around here for me," he'd once said.

I would never comment. I'd just follow him out the door, leaving behind an unfinished meal. So for that reason, he would never know about that part of my life, which I was trying so hard to escape from. I knew if I uttered the word *gay*, he would probably ball up in self-defense, praying that the shit wasn't contagious. That word seemed to make men get all uptight and bent out of shape, as if their manhood were at risk.

Sand had once told me a story about a lesbian femme friend of hers named Ashonda. She'd said Ashonda went to high school with her and had plans to go to college and practice law. One day, Sand, Ashonda, and some of their friends went to a senior ditch party. They were the only sophomores there. They didn't realize that there were only heterosexual people there until all the well-known thugs in the hood started rolling in. She told me that there were these two guys who kept bugging, trying to holler at Ashonda all night. She said Ashonda kept turning them down politely, until they became aggressive. They started calling her out her name and saying shit to her just to get her mad. Ashonda got fed up and pulled out her GAY AND PROUD rainbow bracelet and said, "Look, nigga. I don't do dick. I do pussy."

Everybody in the place started laughing and making fun of them niggas, teasing them about being turned away from some pussy who preferred a pussy. They thought that Ashonda was trying to make fun of them and embarrass them in front of everybody, which was exactly what she did. They waited until she was driving home alone before they raped and killed her. Sand said Ashonda was on the six o'clock news the next morning. Her body was found covered with garbage in an alley.

That was why I was sometimes frightened to go to the gay clubs and attend the rallies and gay pride conventions. When Sand told me that story, it really shook my ass up something good.

I had a stack of lies on top of lies that I had told Vincent. I knew in my heart that I loved Sand, but I also had feelings for my fiancé. He was the man I wanted to be with. Our life together would be more acceptable and promising than mine and Sand's, much more acceptable.

But I was not ready to be up front with Sand, either. She would probably ram my head through a brick wall, with her quick-ass temper. How mad she would be to find out that her gay lover also longed for dick. All those nights of lovemaking with her had played out. Sex with Sand was becoming too predictable. More than that, I was restricted from areas that I had never seen. Sand refused to engage in any type of position that called for her to be on the receiving end. Besides all that, I got tired of giving blow jobs to a toy that couldn't respond with cum in my mouth. I admitted that I was a freak. That was what happened when you were kept in a little shell, protected from the world, never to experience anything or to be able to share experiences. That was what many years in a foster home could do to you. I wanted and needed so badly to be penetrated and touched by a man.

My love nest ached to be pounded by something other than that black rubber dick that Sand strapped around her waist at night.

All this stayed in my mind during my drive back home. It was late, and I knew Sand was probably gon' kick my ass. I unlocked the door and crept on in. I felt like a big-ass teenager sneaking in the house after being warned not to go out, the shit I saw the Huxtable kids do on TV. The hickey on my neck caught her attention. She was looking at me like she wanted to slap the taste right out of my mouth or knock my ass into the middle of next year. I lied through my teeth and told her I had been out running.

Yeah, I'd been running, all right. When I'd seen her walk around that corner as I was pulling up into the apartments, I'd dashed up those steps so fast, you would have thought I was Casper. All you would have seen was my white shirt. I also told her that a mosquito had bitten me. She believed me, I hoped. I couldn't let her figure out what I was doing. We made love later that night. I was tired and had other things running through my mind, but she appeared to be hot and horny. I had to make love to her, or she really would have started putting two and two together. The shit was boring and tiring, but I managed to fake a couple of orgasms in the process.

When that was all said and done, she turned over and went to sleep. I slept next to her, rubbing my belly, trying to bond with my unborn child.

Rene

Today Vincent and I took our first trip to the doctor. It had been exactly one week and three days since I found out I was expecting. I was still in denial and couldn't believe there was actually a baby growing inside of me. Vincent was so excited and was already talking about baby names. I had bigger problems on my mind, and they weren't about trying to decide on a baby name.

Dr. Isaga told me that I was about ten to twelve weeks along, according to my last menstrual. I remembered missing my period for the past two months, but I had just thought that maybe it was from stress. Sand had been stressing lately, trying to get her club ready for opening, and on top of all that, she had found out that her mother had passed away. I knew Sand and her mother weren't close, but I still did not feel like that was a good enough reason for Sand not to pay her respects at her mother's funeral. As much as I had begged and pleaded with her, Sand still hadn't gone. I had even told her I would go with her. Stubborn Sand—that was what I call her now—had still refused. So her stress and worry became mine. Every problem she faced, I had to hear about it.

"Is it a boy or girl?" Vincent was all up in the doctor's face, walking with him side by side, asking him every question that floated off the tip of his tongue. I was sitting in the phlebotomist's chair, about to give four tubes of blood. I closed my eyes and let her stick me for the fifth time.

"You have small veins," she said. "But this one looks good."

"Finally," I mumbled under my breath. She had removed the long rubber band that she'd tied around my arm.

"There you go, Mrs. Montgomery. I'm all done."

I quickly hopped out of that chair and walked back over to my doctor's station. He was chatting with Vincent, the new proud dad.

"So, we will know if it's a boy or a girl in about two more months?" Vincent asked.

"Vincent," I said politely, trying to wave him away from the doctor, who had a room full of patients waiting to be seen. They looked like they were in more need to be seen than I was. One lady looked like she was about to go into labor at any minute. I grabbed Vincent by the arm. "Come on, honey. I'm finished."

He looked at the bandages on my arm. "Ooh, you got a shot."

"I had my blood drawn."

"Same thing," he said, laughing and teasing me.

I still couldn't believe I was having a baby. Me, Rene Brown and soon-to-be Mrs. Montgomery, was about to have a baby. When we got back in the car, I predicted what would go down next.

"Rene, I think we should definitely move the wedding date up." He was driving us back to his house.

"Vincent, how many times do we have to go over this? We can't move the date up. I am still taking care of Grandma, and she needs me."

"Rene, *I* need you. You are pregnant with my baby."

"I know that. You think that I don't?" I asked.

"You don't act like it."

"Honey, I need time to think things out. Everything is just happening a little too fast for me right now."

"Rene, you agreed to marry me. You knew that sooner or later a baby was going to come into the picture. It just happened a little sooner than planned, so what is there to think about?"

"I need to make sure that we do things right. I don't want us to rush into anything."

"What rush? We're having a child. This baby is not gonna wait for us to decide if we're prepared for its arrival. I'm trying to do things right and to marry the woman that I love, who is now the mother of my unborn baby."

I sat there and took in everything Vincent was saying, but still, I was not trying to hear the wedding bells just yet. I knew that things were about to get ugly, so I tried to prevent an argument by staying quiet, letting him do all the talking, like I did when Sand and I got into it.

He continued to fuss. "I can help you find someplace to put your grandmother, if that's what you're worried about."

Listen to him. *Someplace.* If I did have an ill grandmother, and he spoke about her the way he had just spoken, we would be having it out for real. But since it was nothing but a made-up lie, it didn't bother me much.

"We can put her in a nursing home," Vincent continued. "There's one around the corner from the house. That way, she will be close to home, and we can both go see after her every day."

"Vincent, I am not putting my grandma in a nursing home, and that's final. I really don't want to hear anything else about it."

He got quiet. Finally, he looked over at me and asked, "Are you mad?"

"No."

"Do you love me?"

I was speechless, and no words left my lips. I pretended that I didn't hear the question, but I knew he was going to ask it again.

"Rene, did you hear me?"

"Um . . . what? No, baby. I was thinking about names for the baby. If it's a girl, do you like the name Mariah?" I had to flip the script and change the subject to avoid his question about love. Love didn't have anything to do with this right now. If I based my life on who I loved, then I would never be able to leave Sand. That was who I loved. With her was where my heart was.

"Yes, I love that name. Like Mariah Carey, the singer."

"Yes, that's who I was thinking of when it came to mind. Little Mariah. She'll have my long, thick hair, your blue eyes, and pretty, smooth light brown skin."

"Yeah, she's gonna be pretty like her mom," he said.

I couldn't do anything but blush.

"I hope she has your eyes, though," he said as he put the Lincoln Navigator in park and reached over to kiss me. I kissed him back. People were watching us from outside, and they were smiling. I wasn't used to that.

When we got out of the car, his neighbors were waving at us. I waved back, because these folks would soon be my neighbors as well. We walked into the house, and I kicked off my shoes and headed straight for the fridge. I picked up a half gallon of Minute Maid pineapple-orange juice and downed it until the carton was empty.

"Thirsty, are we?"

"Yeah. Very."

He smiled and walked over to me. He kneeled down on the kitchen floor right where I was standing and laid his head on my stomach. "Rene, I need you. I really, really need you."

I ran my fingers through his hair. Vincent was ready to share his life with me, but I wasn't sure if I was ready to share mine with him. I still had unfinished business.

***

When I got back home, Sand was not there. I did remember her telling me that she had to meet with some connects, so I knew it would be late when she got home. This allowed me enough time to do what I needed to do without any interruptions from her.

Vincent had me all wired up, but he had been tripping like hell. Just when I had thought I was about to get me eight inches of some good loving before I left his house, he had pulled away.

"Vincent, what are you doing?" I'd been pulling at his jeans, trying to undress him.

"Rene, I read in one of those baby magazines that it may not be good to have sexual intercourse while you're this early in your pregnancy."

"What?"

"I don't want to hurt the baby."

"Vincent, we can make love. It's okay, I promise you." I tried to slide my hand inside his jeans to see if I could get him hard, but the damn pants were too tight. He still wasn't budging. He knew what I was trying to do and was becoming upset that I was still trying to get my feel on even after he had aired his concerns.

"I don't think we should, honey. Please, respect my wishes." He backed away and re-zipped his fly. I could not believe it. He was dead serious. He was not about to fuck me. I didn't have anything else to say.

When I left his house, I drove straight home. I needed to release some serious tension, and I knew just the thing to do the trick.

My sexual appetite and my desires to be with a man had grown over the years. Sand couldn't fulfill all my desires and sexual fantasies, and I almost felt ashamed for expecting her to.

I retrieved my pink vibrator from the drawer and went to work.

I played all alone until I was too weak and sexually drained to go on. Then I climbed into the bed and drifted off to a lover girl's paradise.

Rene

I was sleeping real good until I heard a loud knock at my door. I knew it wasn't Sand, because she always used her key. It had to be Shun; that was one of her police knocks. I swear, you would have thought she was the police.

"Wait a minute. I'm coming," I yelled from the back room, where I had crashed.

I was still naked from my afternoon escapade. Me and my newfound friends had become real acquainted and were about to meet again just as soon as I could get rid of her ass. I slipped on one of Sand's hooded pullovers and some shorts I often went running in. I went to the door, feeling weak and worn out. I knew the reason but was gonna try damn hard not to let Shun pick up on it. I didn't bother looking out the peephole. I just swung the door open.

The woman before me was not my best friend. I didn't recognize her at all. She was short and petite, with a smooth, clear complexion that any woman would have given up a kidney to have. Her hair was braided and was pulled up into a ponytail. She had on a skintight yellow and hot pink outfit that hugged all her curves. Her sandals and her Coach bag matched perfectly. I thought maybe she was lost and in need of directions, because it seemed like everybody got these damn buildings confused.

"Can I help you with something?" I asked.

She removed the dark-tinted shades from the top of her head and slid them into the side pocket of her purse. "Yes, I believe you can. I'm looking for Sand."

"She's not here right now. May I tell her who stopped by?"

"Do you even *know* where she is right now!" she snapped with an attitude.

"Excuse me?"

"Damn. Now your ass going deaf? I said, Do you even know where your woman is right now? What? You can't comprehend English?"

I stared at the young woman who was posted up in front of me, shifting her head from side to side every time she spoke.

"And who are you?" I asked again with quick boldness.

Shit. I wasn't Sand's keeper, and as far as I was concerned, I had business to take care of before she got back, so this bitch had better make it quick.

"You don't need to be worried about who the fuck I am. I need to talk to her!"

I opened my half-sleepy eyes as wide as they could go. "What did you just say?"

"You heard me. I'm looking for your girlfriend." She was still working her neck from side to side. The bitch really had her nerve. I didn't want any shit, but she was about to make me clown her ass, talking to me like that.

"Look, Sand ain't here! I'll tell her you came by!" I was about to leave her ass standing there, talking to the front of the door. I shifted my foot. "Anything else?" I huffed so she'd get the picture that she was wasting my time.

"You sitting up in there, and you don't have the slightest idea where yo' nigga at right now. That's a damn shame. Do you at least know when she'll be back?"

"Look, I said I don't know where she is, so you need to take your attitude-having ass on and call her on her cell if you need her that damn bad! Who are you, anyway?"

She smirked a little. "That's for me to know and for you to find out." I had had enough of this heifer. I was just about to slam the door in her face, but she blocked it with her foot.

"You need to move your fuckin' foot before I break this bitch," I hissed.

She looked at me as if she dared me to act on my threat. "I wish you would so you can see how deep my other seven and a half can go in your black ass."

I tried forcing the door shut, but her damn foot wouldn't allow the door to close. Plus, I was still weak from the multiple orgasms I had experienced earlier. I still tried, but there was no victory.

"Move, bitch!" I shot back at her.

"What! I know you didn't just call me no bitch, you carpet-munching dyke!"

I hated to be called out of my name, and that word right there was definitely a fighting word. I swung at her ass, and she swung back. Her fake nails flew off, landing north, south, east, and west. She pushed her way inside the apartment. I hit; she swung. She swung, and I ducked. She kicked me in the stomach, and an excruciating pain shot around my abdomen. I kicked and fought my little ass off. She was going for my jaw, but I was able to duck quickly, causing that punch to hit the hard-ass wall. Her knuckles were bleeding, and blood was trickling down from a scratch that I had made on her face.

"Crazy bitch!" I yelled.

When she finally realized her battle was lost, she backed off. Her eyes roamed around my apartment. I was still trying to catch my breath. I bent over, grabbing at my stomach, praying that my baby was unharmed. Before I knew it, she was coming at me with Sand's baseball bat, which she had grabbed from behind the door.

She must have hit me pretty hard, because I lost consciousness. When I came to, I was dizzy but was able to pull myself up from the floor and make my way over to the couch. I was frantic and my head was spinning from the madness. My eyes shot in every direction, looking for the mysterious woman, but she had vanished without a trace. I had a small knot on the back of my head, and it hurt like hell.

I couldn't believe Sand. I couldn't wrap my head around anything that had just happened and the audacity of that bitch to come to my house. I staggered toward the bathroom to check my face. Parts of it felt like they were on fire. I had never had to fight in my life. She could have Sand, if that was what this was all about. My hair was all over my head. The French braid I'd had it in had been torn loose. I looked like a madwoman. I started to call Sand on her cell phone and tell her that it was over, that we were finished. She had just made our breakup so much easier. I decided against it because I wanted to see the look on her face when I told her that she could kiss my black ass good-bye. We were over, and that was for real. I was more than ready to move on with my life. Sand was suddenly my past, a past that I would soon bury.

I dialed Shun's number before I could give in and call Sand. I had to tell her about what had just gone down. The phone just rang. Finally, her oldest son, Jorell, whom everybody called Jo Jo, picked up.

"Jo Jo," I said, "where your mama at?"

"She went to the grocery store with Bubba Earl 'cause we got our food stamps."

"Jo Jo, tell her to come over here when she get in. Tell her it's urgent."

"Okay, Aunt Rene."

He hung up the phone, in a hurry to get back to that video game I could hear his brothers arguing over in the background. I placed the handset back into its cradle. My head was starting to ache again. I went into the kitchen to make an ice pack to place on the swelling area.

Sand was a liar. All this time I had been worried about how she would take me leaving her, and she'd been creeping with hoes behind my back. Doing the same thing I was, being unfaithful. At least I had never brought Vincent into our home. Shit, he didn't even know where I lived. I had made sure I kept my shit together.

She just didn't give a damn. Did she want me to find out? Damn. What was she doing? Calling her tramp over as soon as I left or what? This shit was crazy. A threesome affair had just turned into a foursome. We were all fucking each other unknowingly, carrying on a discreet orgy. If Sand wanted to see other people, all she had to do was say so. It probably wouldn't bother me as much if I had had doubts or had felt like she was cheating, but since I hadn't, this shit was running me wild. Wasn't I enough woman for her? I guessed I just wasn't good enough. She needed cold air to cool her down, and I needed more wood for my fireplace. I had my reasons for stepping out, and as crazy as it sounded, I would have never cheated on Sand with another woman. It wasn't the same. Cheating wasn't just cheating when you were trying to find a substitution to make up for the things you weren't receiving in a relationship. At least that was what I had convinced myself of.

Shun used to ask me how I would know how a real man felt if I had never been with one. She was right. I would have never known if I had allowed Sand to continue to manipulate me like she had done for so many years. I had finally seen the light. All the time I had wasted with her, trying to figure out if I was gay or not, I could have been enjoying a relationship with a *real* man.

A sharp pain stabbed me in the side, and another one shot quickly under my stomach. The pains grew sharper, rushing me without warning. I was hunched over, grabbing at my belly, all while trying to make it back to the bathroom. The urge to pee, vomit, and have a bowel movement came all at once. I sat down on the toilet and pushed. I pushed again, again, and again and finally expelled something from my vagina that didn't feel right. I stood up to see what it was. A stream of blood was flowing from my vagina and down my legs.

"Oh, my God! My baby, my baby," I cried.

I heard the front door open.

"Rene!" Sand called out.

I was still in the bathroom, crying and praying that this was all a dream. *Lord, please let this be a bad dream.* I opened my eyes, and it was not. I sat there on the floor, inhaling the smell of my own puke and feces. Sand had probably just left that bitch's house. The thought of me involuntarily eating another's bitch's pussy off her tongue made me more nauseous than I had been. All those times she was supposed to be with Spliff or James or at the fucking club . . . It was all a lie. I couldn't believe I had let her do this to me. But it had worked out in my favor. She could move on with her life, and I could move on with mine. An eye for an eye. I was ready to pack my shit and bounce.

Sand came into the bathroom.

"You all right?" she asked, eyeing me strangely.

I clutched my stomach.

"You cramping?" she asked.

I gave her the silent treatment. She picked me up, took me into the bedroom, and undressed me. Then she ran me a warm bubble bath and placed me in the tub.

I kept my silence for the rest of the night, while she pretended like there wasn't a damn thing wrong. I wanted to cuss her ass out and demand that she tell me about the bitch she was fucking behind my back. I wanted to know what her reason was for cheating on me, because I had plenty to support why I was. But I had had enough drama for one day. I didn't have shit to say to her, and as far as I was concerned, she didn't have shit to say to me, either.

As I glared at her from across the kitchen table, I realized that I had been trapped. Caught up in a world that I had never belonged in—a world where I had been kept as Sand's prisoner. It sickened me, the eye contact she made with me, as if things were so peachy between the two of us. She played her role real well.

"Rene, baby, what's wrong? Are you feeling okay?" Boy, did she need a standing ovation for her performance.

I stared at the box that contained the dinner she had ordered. I didn't lift a finger.

"Aww," I moaned. Another excruciating pain was stabbing me below my pelvis. I braced myself and exhaled.

"You all right?" she asked me again.

I rolled my eyes at her, stood up, and slowly walked back into the bedroom. Another pain nearly brought me to my knees.

Sand

Jasmine was still calling and blowing up my phone like crazy. Every time she called. I would hang up, and she would call right back. She had left an ugly message on my voice mail today that made me wanna go over to her place and kick her ass.

"Sand, you know who this is. I'm tired of you hanging up the damn phone in my face! You weren't playing that role when your ass was in between my legs, eatin' this pussy, now were you? I knew you were gonna come back. Talking about you wanted to leave the night at the party where it was. *Please*. You are the one that called me, asking if you could come through. Not me, but you, Sand! Baby, I know this pussy good, and the same way you called me, asking if you could come through, is the same way I'm calling you, letting you know I wanna fuck. I need my pearl tongue licked. This ain't no muthafuckin' 'have it Sand's way.' I guess you think you can just come through when you want to or when you need a quickie. Uh-uh. It don't even work like that. You better have your ass over here no later than ten p.m., or else. Tell that ho of yours that you got plans. You gonna have to be on my time tonight." *Beep*. "End of message."

She had surely lost her everlasting mind. I had deleted that shit as soon as I heard it. If Rene got ahold of my phone and heard that, all hell would break loose.

Jasmine had me fucked up if she thought she was running shit. Trying to call me out. Better yet, threaten me. She wanted to turn psycho on me and show her true colors after realizing that I wasn't ever gonna leave Rene for her ass. She wanted more from me than what I was willing to give. She wasn't shit but a quick lay for me. Ain't no telling how many niggas she was fucking with, because I knew she wasn't 429—*gay*. I couldn't believe I was dealing with some deranged, Sand-whipped crazy head. I went on trying to forget about the other night. I admitted that I was horny as fuck that night, and at that time Rene was being a little distant. So that night Jasmine was the only person I could think of who wouldn't have a problem with me coming through. But now I knew that was a big-ass mistake. And she proudly threw that night up in every damn message she left on my phone.

My club was almost finished, and the grand opening was going to be on Saturday. I had plenty of talent coming through. I had set up twelve live performances. I had local artists who were on the grind, out pushing their CDs for ten dollars a cop, coming through. This would be their shot at getting their name out there, plus some free promotion. I also had invited some of the popular DJs and radio producers who I knew had major connections to the big shots. Everybody was gonna be in the place. The word had spread, and Sandrene's was going to be the place to be on Friday and Saturday nights. The doors would open at nine and wouldn't close until five.

I had to make sure that I was extra fly, so that meant hitting up the mall. Everything I saw and liked, I bought. I even picked Rene up a few things. I was loaded with bags as I walked out of the stores. I climbed in my car and put in a CD that I had just bought from a cat yesterday, while I was washing my ride. His name was Vic Damon. I turned the volume up and bumped it all the way home. The tracks were hitting hard, and that female that he had on there was spitting it like the next Mia X. I was low profiling all the way back to the house. Every time I stopped at a light, I would attract major attention. I wasn't sure if it was the spree wheels I had on Ms. Lady that was attracting the attention or the new chameleon-colored paint job my boy Sergio had had Carlos hook me up with. My ride was lime green, purple, and royal blue, and at night it was camouflage navy. *Hot damn! Cleaner than a muthafucka.*

My cell was once again ringing off the hook. I regretted giving my number to Jasmine, because that was whose number popped up on the caller ID. As many times as she called me, there was no excuse for me not to know her shit by memory. I didn't answer. I almost did on that last ring so I could chin check that ass. Thinking about her past calls and her voice-mail messages made me mad all over again. I wanted to go in the opposite direction and set her ass straight. Instead, I leaned back, trying to enjoy the breeze as I Cadillac'd through the inner-city streets of D-Town.

It was normally steaming hot around this time of day, but today was breezy and nice out. I thought about how only a few years ago, I'd been homeless. No place to sleep, no car to ride around in, and broke like a joke. I had been doing anything and everything I could to make a dollar. I had even sold that yay yo for a hot minute. I'd sold nickel and dime sacks to anybody and everybody who had the funds to buy it. Stooping to levels that I would not have had to go if it weren't for Ruby Mae, the woman who had called herself my mother. The woman who had kicked me out into the streets, with no money for food. I remembered that day like it was yesterday.

I came home from school all excited because I had received my TAAS results. I had all passing scores.

"Mama, where you at? I wanna show you something." I looked around the entire house for her. I knew she had to be home, because she didn't work or drive, so there was no other place for her to be but in the house, cooking or cleaning. "Mama," I kept yelling at the top of my lungs. "I gotta show you something."

I headed for my room, hoping that she had not gotten comfortable there. I shot up the stairs.

"Mama."

She was sitting on my bed, with her face buried in a letter. There were other letters surrounding her, apparently those that she had already read and chucked to the side. I saw that my white, red, and blue K-Swiss box was open. That was where I kept all my letters that were supposed to be secret and for my eyes only. Letters from my first girlfriend, Deandra. Mama had violated my space. Trespassed. Overstepped the boundaries that I felt I was entitled to have. When she heard my voice, she placed the white piece of paper in her lap. She had tears running down her face. I already knew what letter she had found.

"Mama," I kept saying. "Why are you in my room, in my things?"

She walked up to me slowly, holding the letter in her left hand. She raised her right hand, and a forceful slap stung my face. I grabbed at the stinging pain that shot through the left side of my jaw, numbing the entire half of my face. Tears fell from my eyes.

"How could you do this to me?" She held the letter up in my face.

"What, Mama? Do what?"

"So you dyking now? You trying to be one of them there funny people? You're in love with some girl that has the same thing in between her legs as you do? Damn you, Cassandra! You're a disgrace! I went through nine hours of hard labor to give you life, and this is how you repay me?"

I stood there, face-to-face with my mother. She was still crying, allowing me to witness the tears free-fall from her eyes onto the paper.

She shook her head. "This is nonsense, Cassandra. How long? When? Why? I thought we raised you better than this."

I couldn't reply. I was too mad at her for fumbling through my things. Almost ashamed that she had to find out about me this way. But why was she even in my room to begin with, searching through my personal belongings? "Mama, why were you going through my stuff?"

"Do you pay the goddamned bills around here? Huh? Do you? Hell, no you don't! I can look and go through whatever the hell I want to go through in this damn house as long as my name is Ruby Mae Ross!"

Spit flew from her mouth and landed in my face. I wiped it away, scared to make any sudden moves. Afraid she would slap the shit out of me again. The last time she had knocked my ass clean across the room with a one hitter quitter. She had thought I was trying to buck up to fight after she had worn my big ass out with an extension cord. Bad grades and that was the ultimate down-home ass beating.

"I want you to get your shit and get the fuck out my house!" Her loud yells sent chills through my body. I walked to my closet to grab the few clothes that were hanging from the racks. "Uh-uh. What are you doing?"

"I'm getting my clothes, like you told me to."

"Like hell you are! You're not taking a damn thing that me and your father bought! I mean get your slutty filth. The shit you've been hiding in that there closet!" She threw the letter at me that she held in her hand. She pointed to the open shoe box on my bed. "I want that shit out my house right goddamned now, and you along with it!"

"Mama, where am I gonna go? I don't have anywhere to go." I was begging for her to take back the threat of putting me out in the streets. She didn't. "Mama, please!" I begged, crying like a little girl. "I ain't got nowhere to go."

"I don't give a damn where you go. Long as you ain't here. I don't wanna ever see your face round here. And don't bother comin' round me. You're dead, you hear me? Dead!"

I grabbed my knapsack and the box of letters that revealed the life that I lived outside of my parents' home. The life that I had chosen to keep a deep, dark secret.

As I walked down the steps, I saw my dad standing at the bottom of them, his head bowed down, unable to look me in the face.

"Daddy?"

"Just leave, Sand." I could still hear the cries that came from my upstairs room. "Just leave and do what your mother asks."

My dad never looked up, and I never looked back. I just headed out the door to face what was coming to me.

From that day on, my life changed for the better. I wanted to be accepted for who I was, not for who someone wanted me to be. I lived my life the way I wanted to live it. When I left that house, I left knowing that I would probably never see my mother and father again. As long as my name was Cassandra Janene Ross, that would be all right by me.

I pulled up into the reserved parking space in front of my building. Rene's car was there, so she was upstairs. I gathered all the bags and walked up the flight of stairs.

"Rene," I called out when I stepped through the front door.

She didn't answer back.

I put down the bags, which seemed as if they weighed a hundred pounds in all. I heard sniffles coming from the bathroom. I walked in, and there was Rene, bent over the toilet, vomiting.

"What's wrong, baby?" Her eyes were red, and her hair was all out of place. The puke made my stomach turn once the strong smell hit my nostrils. I slipped off my jersey and helped her up from the floor. "What's wrong, baby?" I asked again.

She refused to look me in the face. She just continued to sit on the rug and stare at the porcelain toilet.

I grabbed a white washcloth from under the sink, along with some of her personal bathing items. I wiped her mouth. She wasn't talking, just staring into thin air. I ran her a warm bath with bubbles and aromatherapy bath beads. Maybe she was coming down with the flu or something, I thought.

"Rene, what's wrong? Did you get ahold of some bad food or something?"

She didn't respond.

I flushed the toilet and closed the lid. Then I checked her forehead for a fever. I carried her into the bedroom and removed all her clothes. Then I carried her back into the bathroom. I gently sat her down in the tub, then stripped from head to toe, leaving nothing but my boxer shorts on. I climbed in behind her and wiped her body down like she was a two-year-old child. She was still quiet. I rubbed her neck, her breasts, and ran the washcloth down the center of her back. After I bathed her, I ordered her favorite Chinese dinner. After the food was delivered, she just sat and stared at it like she had never seen such a dish before.

"Are you gonna eat?" I asked.

She shot me a look that could kill.

"What's up with you?" I said.

"I'm not hungry."

She stood up from the table and started for the bedroom, leaving her food untouched. Minutes later she had fallen asleep. I stayed up watching late-night videos on MTV.

It was 11:56 p.m. when our doorbell rang. I looked out the peephole, and Miss Shun was knocking on the door and ringing the doorbell at the same time. This maniac was about to get cussed the hell out. I opened the door before she could break it down.

She barged in. "Where is she?"

"She's in the room." My face suggested the mood I was in. And to make matters worse, I had to see her ass.

She had on her pajamas, and a plastic cap covered her out-of-date Jheri curl. She ran toward the bedroom, causing the pictures and mirrors on the wall to shake. I followed her.

"Rene, are you all right, honey? I came as soon as I got your message."

"What message?" I asked, confused about what was going on.

Nobody bothered to answer me. I stood there and watched how Shun embraced my woman, comforting her in her big arms. She was rocking her back and forth, and Rene was crying, letting out emotions that she had not shown me earlier.

"What's wrong with her?" I asked Shun.

She looked at me with a frown on her face and a look of disgust. She rolled her big-ass eyes at me. I stood at the bedroom door, looking helpless and confused. Shun pulled the comforter back on the bed and allowed Rene to free herself from the covers.

"What are you doing? She was resting," I said.

"Cassandra, you are so damn clueless."

"What!"

Shun walked past me, and Rene followed behind her.

"Rene, where are you going?" I watched my baby as she walked in front of me, heading toward the front door.

"Can't you see she need a damn doctor?"

"I can take her, then," I said. "That's my job. I don't need you doing that when I can. Rene is my woman, not yours."

"Humph. And you're so sure." Shun shook her head and smirked.

"What the fuck is that supposed to mean, Shun?"

"Never mind me. She doesn't want you there."

Ignoring Shun, I turned to face Rene, who was almost out the door. I quickly walked over to her. "Rene, baby, you don't want me to go?"

She looked at me with so much hurt and pain in her eyes. "No, Sand. Please stay."

I was hurt, but I respected her wishes. It was nothing but a little cold. Or maybe she was coming down with the flu or something. I knew she would be all right. It was nothing major, I hoped. I kissed her on the forehead, but she turned away at my touch. Why in the hell was she acting so cold toward me all of a sudden? Something wasn't right, and I could feel it. I stepped outside and watched Shun speed away with my woman leaning on her shoulder.

I went back inside, and the clock radio read 12:20 a.m. I was tired, but my mind was processing a million thoughts per second. Twenty minutes later, my cell phone started ringing. I hoped that it was Shun, letting me know that she and Rene had made it to the emergency room, which was about ten minutes up the street. The number displayed was listed as unknown. I normally didn't answer calls from unknown numbers, since I had a crazy head calling me, but this late at night, I knew it couldn't have been anyone other than Shun or Rene.

"Hello."

"What's up, baby?"

"Who is this?"

"Don't act like you don't know my voice by now." The attitude sounded familiar. "Look out your window."

I walked over to the blinds, opened them a tad bit to see if there was anyone outside. I saw no one. "Look, whoever the fuck you are, you about to get this phone hung up in your face and you can talk to the dial tone."

"Don't you see me?"

I continued examining the parking lot, using my twenty-twenty vision. I finally spotted a female figure standing near my baby Lady. My precious car.

"Okay, I'll give you a hint. My pussy is shaved in an S."

I almost dropped the phone. Now I could make out the fake-ass voice she was trying to disguise with a low seductive one. It was Jasmine. The bitch was stalking me. And how the hell did she know where I lived?

"Jasmine, what the fuck do you want? And how your ass know where I live?"

"Don't worry. Don't worry. Ain't nobody stalkin' you. My brother lives across the street. I was just over there delivering something to him, and I just happened to spot your car."

"Why are you even calling me?" I asked, not believing or buying into any of her bullshit. "I told your ass I ain't feeling you no more," I blurted into the phone.

She started laughing. "Sand, don't try and act like you don't miss me. You know you like the way I back this thang up. I bet your bitch can't make that ass clap like mine. I've left you messages. I know you got 'em."

"Yeah, I got 'em, and I can't believe you were bold enough to leave that shit on my muthafuckin' voice mail."

"Ooh, sounds like big daddy mad. I'm shaking in my thong, I'm so scared." She was laughing at me like I had just said some hilarious-ass shit. "Sand, what makes you think you can just start something and not finish it? You got me all fucked up."

This bitch was certified crazy. I wasn't about to stay on the phone and listen to her deranged ass. "Jasmine, I ain't got time for this childish-ass shit you playing. What you want from me, huh? You need money, some clothes, shoes? What? Goddamn, what it take to keep your ass from calling me and poppin' up all over the place?" My voice grew louder. "Damn, go find you another mutha-fucka to harass!"

I continued to watch from the blinds. I could see her silhouette bent over on my ride.

"Bitch, don't fuck with my car!"

I wanted to run down there and kick her ass, but I knew that if I walked out that door, her ass was gon' get more than kicked. I was goin' to stomp a big pothole in her ass. Fucking with Ms. Lady was a fat-ass no-no. That was one thing I didn't play around with nobody threatening. My ride was my everything. Ms. Lady was my main bitch, ahead of everything else.

"Fuck this damn car!"

"Good. Yeah, fuck the car and fuck me. Now, get the hell on, you crazy bitch."

That's what I get for falling for her immature ass.

"Bitch? Oh, so now I'm a bitch? You know what? I got your bitch. I bet you won't be talking all that shit when your little wifey find out that you been coming over to my place when she won't give you no pussy. I bet you won't have shit to say then, huh? You ain't seen crazy yet! You fucked with the wrong one. I'll show your ass crazy, if that's what you wanna see!" *Click.*

I waited about an hour before I went down to check on my car. I didn't wanna take any chances on running into Jasmine's psychotic ass.

Ms. Lady was fine and in the same condition I had left her in. She was waxed down from head to toe, with accessorized blingage to go along. There wasn't a week that went by that I didn't take her down to my boy Sergio to get primped up. He'd whip her ass up real good, then send her home to Papa. She had screens in each headrest, a plush interior, and was wood grained out. It was like she was a necessity to me. She was my accomplice and my roll dawg. She put niggas in check as soon as she opened her mouth, and her presence alone demanded full attention. She commanded respect when she stepped on the scene and was pregnant with an engine that melted them haters. Her voice was deep with a heavy bass, and every word that she spoke was a tune you could bob to. My bitch was bad, classy, and hella seductive. Ms. Lady was the shit, and not too many niggas could fuck with her around the block.

I surfed my cell, deleting all that crazy bitch's messages and phone numbers. I had fourteen missed calls, and they were all from her stupid, childish ass. Whatever the hell I had got myself into, it was serious. This bitch was about to cause me some problems. I just knew it. I thought back to the night I last saw that crazy-ass girl.

"What's up, Jasmine? Are you busy?"

"No, baby, but you were just on my mind. What are you doing?"

"Shit. Just trying to come through, if that's all right with you."

"You know I ain't tripping, but ain't your girl gonna be looking for you?"

"Nah. I told her I was gon' chill out at one of my partners' house tonight."

"Damn. And she cool with that shit?"

"Yeah. We going through it right now, and she ain't been feeling too good, anyway. Why you asking me twenty-one damn questions? You got somebody up over there? Do I need to keep heading home?"

"Hell, nah. Ain't nobody up in here. If you coming, come on."

I busted a big-ass U-turn in the middle of the lane. I wasn't about to miss out on an opportunity like this. All she had to do was say the word. Plus, Rene had been tripping hella hard lately. She had been acting real funny and always complaining about every little single thing. It seemed like she was PMSing every damn day of the week. She woke up with a 'tude and lay down with one. I figured I'd give her a day to herself so she could chill the fuck out with the mood swings.

Jasmine was fine as hell and as enticing as they came. She came to the door in a sexy red negligee with some slide-in matching house shoes, smelling like White Diamonds perfume. Her hair was done in small tight curls. She threw herself at me the moment I appeared in the doorway. I was about to speak, but she silenced me, answering the question I had written on my face before letting me open my mouth. Her long-ass tongue was damn near down my throat, and her free hand found its way under my shirt. I grabbed on to her soft ass, gently gripped it, and gave it a couple of powerful smacks.

When I finally made my way in the door, I saw how she'd taken the time to light candles, burn incense, and put on soft jazz music. The mood was set, and I had all that I needed to work with right in front of me, waiting to be bent over and spanked in the worst way. She was thick as a loaf of bread and sharper than a fresh blade. Slick and full of mystique.

"I got something I wanna show you," she said seductively. She took small baby steps backward and awarded me with the benefit of a full view of her scrumptious Coke bottle figure. She removed her nightgown, letting it ease down to the hardwood floor. She was standing in front of me, bare, in nothing but her brown skin. I walked toward her, trying to make out what it was she was pointing to down below her pubic area. I was like, "Whoa!" when I seen the shit. I knew then this broad was on some psychotic shit for real. Her pussy hairs had been trimmed and neatly shaven into an S.

"What the hell is that?" I asked her.

"It's your initial. You like?"

Now, I could have done one of two things. I could have torn the damn hinges off that door, trying to get away from her ass, or I could have done what I did. Stayed there and got what I had driven way across town for . . . some pussy.

I regretted like all hell going over to her place that night. I should have just taken my horny ass home. Instead, I had let my hormones once again get the best of me. When I had spotted June Bug, who lived across the street, coming out of her place that night, I had automatically assumed her ass was fucking with guys right off the bat. I was about to bounce but wanted to catch her in the act of trying to play this two-way game with me. *What she got to say now*? I thought, knocking and ringing her doorbell a few times. I knew she had heard me when I hit the neighborhood. Ms. Lady announced herself on every block I strolled through. I had seen June Bug come out of her apartment with my own two eyes, and I knew he recognized my car. But before I opened my mouth to drill her, she opened the door and stopped me.

"That's my brother, so don't even trip. He was stopping by to bring me something."

Small-ass world, I thought. If only he knew that his baby sister was a freaky bitch who fucked with niggas like me.

The next morning I woke up alone in the queen-size sleigh bed I shared with Rene. She had still not made it home from the hospital, and no one had bothered even to call me to give me her status. I had already made my mind up that I was going to go to the hospital, anyway, to check on her, regardless of whether she wanted me to or not. She hadn't even told me why she didn't want me there in the first place. I guessed it was just a woman thing, and I would bet my bottom dollar that Shun's ass was not gonna pick up the phone to call me to release me from my worry. I would have been the last person on her list to contact if needed. But I was sure everything had to be fine.

I jumped in my car and headed for my club. I wanted to make sure everything was coming along as planned. I drove through about six lights until I reached Martin Luther King, Jr. Boulevard. I made a left, and when I pulled up in the parking lot, I could see that my employees were working and not jiving around on my time and money. Some were working on outside light fixtures, and some were inside adding the finishing touches. The club was near completion, and I couldn't have been more proud of how it had turned out. Rene was going to be in shock. I hadn't talked about the club for weeks. She had no idea that it was nearly completed. This was all for her. My money, my time were all wrapped up in this building so that I could take things to another level.

When I left the club, it was about three o'clock in the afternoon. I drove to a common spot in Pleasant Grove where I used to get my fade done up. I let this female whom I used to watch braid hair braid me up. She looked good too, but she wasn't down with my type. I could sense it without having to ask. She was real cool, laid back, and down to earth, a character when she wanted to be. She always had niggas laughing and shit. Loved the attention. She didn't take no shit, and you should have heard how she chin checked those niggas in the shop, putting every single one of them in their place. She was the only female up in there holding it down with the fades, cuts, braids, whatever you wanted. She did the fellas and the ladies, but her expertise was in braiding.

I sat back in the reclined chair and lowered my head into the washbowl. She washed my hair and massaged my scalp. I had to give it everything I had to maintain my composure, because she was working one of my spots, my head.

"So how long have you been braiding your hair?" she asked me.

"It's been a while now."

I wondered if she remembered me from when I had the bald fade and the trimmed sideburns. When I'd come to town to see Rene, I would come through to get faded by the best barber in D-Town before heading back to school.

"So, do you have a braider, or do you just let anybody play in your head?" she asked.

I almost said something that would have probably got my ass put out of the shop. Instead of risking it, I just told her that my girl normally braided my hair. She kept doing what she did, and I sat back and watched the other barbers do their thang. When she was finished, I slid her a C-note. She handed me a handheld mirror so I could check out the artwork in the back. She was definitely something serious. She had braids going every which way.

"This tight," I said, complimenting her.

She handed me two twenty-dollar bills and a ten.

"Uh-uh. What you doin'?"

"Here's your change."

"Nah, that's for you, baby girl. Keep that."

"All right. 'Preciate ya," she said. She tucked the fifty dollars back in her bra and swung the cape from around my shoulders. "Do you need me to schedule you for an appointment one week from today?"

"Nah. My girl should be feeling better by then, but if you have a card, I'll keep it handy, just in case."

She reached into her brown apron and pulled out one of her personalized business cards. She handed it to me, and I slid it in my back pocket.

"By the way, do you go out?" I asked.

"I get out sometimes. That's if I can get my kids' daddy to babysit they bad asses. Why you ask?"

"Well, my new club is opening this Saturday, and I was going to give you a VIP pass to come check it out."

"Okay. It doesn't look like I'm gonna be that booked up, anyway, so I'll see if I can make it through."

"Okay. Let me grab some passes out the car."

I went back out to my car and found two VIP passes. I went back inside, wrote my name on the back of the passes, and handed them to her. "Here you go. One for you and one for a friend that you might want to bring along." I watched her look over the purple tickets, which exempted her and a buddy from the twenty-dollar cover charge, plus gave them free admission into the VIP.

"All right. I'm sure I'll be able to make something happen. Thanks."

"Cool. I'll see you then." I turned away but then quickly turned back. "It's Nessa, right?"

"You got it."

"Thanks for my hair."

I walked back outside and passed the bootleg CD man, the stolen cell phones pusher, and the old woman selling barbecue plates with potato salad and beans for eight bucks. I hopped in my ride and turned the music back up once I drove out of the parking lot. I glanced down at my cell, and there were still no calls from Rene. I was starting to worry all over again, so I decided not to delay my visit to the hospital any longer.

I pulled up into the Baylor University Medical Center parking garage. I walked into the building and searched for a help desk or a patient information booth. I spotted a help desk and hurried over.

"Excuse me, ma'am," I said to the woman behind the desk. "Could you tell me where I can find a patient by the name of Rene Brown?"

"Yes, sir. Do you know if she was brought in through the emergency?"

"Yes, ma'am. She came in last night."

The brown-skinned woman was tapping away on a keyboard and looking over the spectacles that rested on her narrow nose. She reminded me of Ruby Mae in a way, except this woman was older. She wore her hair in a French roll with swooping bangs. She was real pretty, just like my mother. She had the wide hips, the high cheekbones, and the thickness that came along with her black heritage. Although she resembled my mother greatly, she didn't dress like her. Her coordinated outfit was not at all appealing. She had on a mint-green pleated skirt with a yellow blouse and some peanut butter–colored walking shoes. She was neat, but talk about tacky. Her grandkids needed they ass whupped for letting her walk out the damn house like that. My moms had shopped out of the JCPenney catalog, and if it hadn't looked right on the models, she sure as hell hadn't bought it. Lord rest her soul.

"Sir, did you say Rene Brown?"

"Yes, ma'am."

"I'm sorry, but I don't have a Rene Brown in my computer. Are you sure of the last name? Because I have a Rene Montgomery, but not a Brown."

"No, I'm sure it's Brown. That's my girlfr . . ." I stopped in mid-sentence. I had to catch myself, because I respected my elders, and had she known I was a woman, I would never have told her that Rene was my girlfriend. But since she thought I was a man, I finished what I had to say. "That's my girlfriend. She was brought in late last night."

"I'm sorry, sir. I'm not showing a Rene Brown checked in. Maybe she went to a different hospital."

I was sure she'd come here. After all, this hospital was the closest. "That's okay. I'll call later." Maybe they hadn't put her in the computers yet, I figured.

I walked out of the building. When I got back to the crib, I got out the phone book and dialed every hospital in Dallas that I could think of. No one had a patient by the name of Rene Brown. I searched the caller ID for Shun's number. When I needed to see her number on the damn thing, it wasn't there. There were two numbers, though, that were displayed under pay phone. I checked the messages, but there still weren't any. I hoped those pay phone calls had not come from Rene, but if they had, she would have known to hit me on the cellular, or she would at least have left a message letting me know she was fine.

I knew she would call again, so I waited, rolled me a sticky icky, and puffed, puffed passed the fuck out.

Sand

My cell was vibrating on my hip. I flipped it open, and the word across the screen read unavailable.

"Hello," I answered.

No reply from the other end.

"Rene?" I blurted. "Is this you?"

Still nothing but silence.

I walked to the front door of the apartment, trying to get a better signal. I got the same silent treatment. Suddenly, I heard "Twisted," by Keith Sweat, playing from somewhere inside the apartment. I followed the sound back to the bedroom. The tune became clearer as I approached the bedroom door. I walked in, trying to determine exactly where the sound was coming from. I spotted Rene's brown purse on the bedside nightstand.

I looked through the purse, searching for the ringing cell phone. I found nothing. It had to be nearby. I looked behind the headboard, under the bed, and even shuffled through the sheets. Still no cell. The phone had stopped ringing, and now I could hear the missed call alert indicating there was an unanswered call. I pulled back the sliding door of the closet, where usually all our clothes were neatly hung separately and our shoes were neatly stacked. The clothes that should have been hanging from hangers were not. They were piled up on the floor, in one tall stack.

What the fuck was this all about?

All the clothes I had spent my hard-hustled money on were on the floor. This shit hadn't been this way when I left the apartment earlier in the day. Someone had been up in here, but no one else had the key or access to this apartment except for Rene. I couldn't understand it. Why would she do this? This wasn't at all like her.

I heard the message alert sound again. I had almost forgotten the reason I was standing in the closet to begin with. I pushed all the clothes to the side, because the ringing noise was coming from underneath the pile. And there it was, the pink fur case that held the electronic device that Rene and I often communicated through. I picked it up and flipped it open. I was going to trace back the last call. I hoped it was Rene. The shit was odd, but I didn't think that much about it. I was still partially buzzed, and thinking was not what I was trying to do right now. I was trying to find my girl; that was all.

I hit the OUTGOING AND INCOMING HISTORY button. There were numerous calls made to one number in particular. Six and seven calls back-to-back. Incoming and outgoing. I raised my brow, making a mental note of the 2:00 a.m. call. Who in the hell was she calling at that hour? I hit the MISSED HISTORY button. The call that had just been made was from an anonymous caller. The time read 5:32 p.m. There was no way to find out who it was. Now I was getting pissed, because lately that was all I was seeing— private calls, anonymous calls, unavailable calls, pay phone numbers, unknown area codes. The only thing different was that this call had been made to Rene's cell phone, and not to mine or the home phone.

I was about to put the phone back in Rene's purse when it started to ring again. I flipped it back open, and I couldn't have grabbed my keys and headed out that door fast enough. A clear picture of Jasmine emerged on Rene's phone screen. She looked the same way she had that night I went over to her crib. As a matter of fact, that was exactly how she had looked when I went over there. She had on that same red gown, and her hair was styled in the same short cut.

This bitch had set me up. She was playing me like a muthafucka. Ain't no telling how long I'd been a part of this fucked-up game she had going. I had to find Rene. What if she had seen that shit on her phone? Maybe that was why she'd ripped the clothes off the racks. Maybe she had spoken with Jasmine. Maybe Jasmine had told her all the shit I did that night at James's house or, better yet, that night at her place.

Jasmine was about to get hurt. I had tried to play calm, but now she had overstepped her fuckin' boundaries. How the fuck had her picture got on Rene's cell phone in the first place? I had to find out what and who I was dealing with.

I was already in my car and down the street. I didn't know what I was capable of at this point, but I did know that it was something serious. I headed back to the place where it had all begun. The odd look. The sly smile. And then the phone number written in red, which had eventually led to more than what I'd anticipated. Sophisticated Images. I pulled up in front of Jasmine's place of employment. I didn't see her car. She had a burgundy 2003 Chevy Malibu, and there was no Malibu in sight. I drove around the building twice.

I spotted the short Asian man who had taken my and Rene's pictures. He had a brown briefcase in his hand and was walking toward a charcoal-gray SUV. I pulled up alongside him, and he started walking faster when he saw me roll up with dark-tinted windows. I rolled down my driver's side window so he could see me better, maybe even recognize me. After all, I had spent a total of $161.00 on some damn pictures that were still sitting around the house.

"Excuse me, sir, but I'm looking for an employee of yours."

He wouldn't stop, just walked even faster, hoping to make it to his vehicle safe and unharmed. I knew he was scared as fuck. A young nigga like me creeping on the lot of his business, looking like he 'bout to pull a kick doe, was intimidating. He probably had much cash on him too. That was why his ass started picking up speed a little bit more, until he was damn near skipping. He hopped in his van and sped away.

I waited in the lot a little bit longer. The wait was gonna be well worth it. I was goin' to kick Jasmine's ass from here all the way to her house. I was gonna fuck her ass up.

The sun had gone down, and it was already dark. I knew Jasmine had to be in there. She had told me once that she usually didn't leave work until about eight o'clock. It was ten minutes to. I started to go in but stopped myself. I didn't want anyone to call the law for the domestic dispute they were bound to report on me. I waited a while longer. I saw everyone leaving and jumping into their cars, everyone except for Jasmine. I circled the building once again. It was now 8:15 p.m., and Jasmine still had not come out. Maybe her little ass was hiding inside, watching me, getting a thrill at my expense. *Fuck it.* I'd show her who to play games with.

I drove to her house. I knocked on the door just to make sure that she and I would be the only ones in the place. No one answered. I gripped the door handle, looked around to be sure no one was in sight, and then used my hips to force my way in.

"What the fuck!"

Candles were burning, and wax drippings had collected beneath them. Had I not come in, something would have caught fire and turned her little town house to ashes. I blew each of them out. Someone had to be in here. I peeked into each one of the rooms cautiously. I didn't need any surprises. I found my way to her bedroom, where I had once laid my head. I wished I could delete the horrible memory from my mind, but I couldn't. It would be there forever. I felt like I had been branded, and the scratches that were still on my backside proved it.

I made my way through the house. I stopped near the bathroom when I heard the shower running. The door was partially closed. I could smell citrus-scented vapors overlapping the scent of honeydew candles that flowed all through the house. I opened the bathroom door, eased my way inside, ready to choke the shit out of Jasmine's ass. Heat and steam from the hot water fogged the mirrors. I made my way closer, stepping over towels and plastic trash bags that were laid out across the floor. I could see the shadow of Jasmine in the shower, but it looked like she was sitting down in the tub.

I was careful and made sure not to make any noises. I walked even closer. I snatched back the shower curtain, causing the holders to fall to the floor. My eyes grew big, and my chest tightened. I tried covering my face with my forearm. The image was far more disturbing than any movie or newscast I had ever seen. The shit was real, and although Jasmine had caused me major problems, I still found myself feeling somewhat sorry for her, maybe even a little hurt.

Her eyes told it all.

Jasmine was dead. I couldn't believe it. Somebody had killed her.

Out of all the shit I had seen in my life, this was the worst. I'd seen a fiend get kicked around and shot at, but not killed. I had even seen a homeless man run into the middle of the street, in front of a moving city bus, attempting to commit suicide. His attempt had failed. Everyone had watched as he'd lain there, paralyzed, blood pouring from his skull as he spoke in a language that sounded foreign. Three weeks later I'd passed him on the street. Only this time he was in a wheelchair and had an amputated leg and bandages around his forehead. Sometimes the homeless did crazy shit like that. Some of them wanted off the streets so bad that if it meant killing themselves or robbing a convenience store to be put in a jail cell, where they were guaranteed something to eat and somewhere to lie, then that was the choice they would make. Out of all the things I'd ever witnessed with my own two eyes, nothing had ever prepared me for some shit like that.

I wasn't even trying to see Jasmine like that. Her lifeless body lay in a tub of running hot water. She was naked. Her eyes were partially open. I moved in closer to see if she had been shot or stabbed. There were no stab wounds and no bullet holes. There wasn't even any blood. Her mouth was crooked, and it looked like she had something inside of it. I was face-to-face with her corpse.

As I moved closer to her, trying to see what it was that had caused her mouth to inflate, I realized it was something black. I separated her lips more. I pulled at the material that had been stuffed in her mouth and practically forced down her throat. Her body tilted over, and her head fell into my chest. I laid her back, still shocked and terrified at the sight of her. I finally got a grip on the black cloth that had been crammed in her windpipe. I eased it out while scrunching my nose up, trying not to inhale the strong vapors that came from the material. It was Jasmine's underwear.

The fumes from the panties burned my nostrils. Just to be sure, I brought the underwear closer to my nose, and the smell was what I had suspected it was . . . gasoline.

I was shook up. I tried to regain my composure, but I couldn't. I left Jasmine's body the same way I had discovered it. Someone had killed her and had left her body to burn. They had lit candles, knowing the place would catch fire. And to make sure she burned up along with it, they had saturated her underwear with gasoline and stuffed it down her throat. As much as I hated Jasmine for the shit she had done and had tried to do, I still couldn't help feeling bad for her. She didn't deserve to go out like that. I wondered if there was someone out there whom she had beef with. Or it could have been one of those sex offenders who had been on the news, the ones women were being warned about.

Whoever the perpetrator was, they knew Jasmine, because there were no signs of a forced entry prior to my intrusion. I thought about someone following her to her apartment and knocking her out cold. After that maybe they raped her before murdering her, and then they tried to set the place on fire so there would be no evidence. I thought about all types of shit that could have possibly happened to her before she died. The scary scenarios just fucked with me more than seeing Jasmine like that.

It was a little after nine in the morning. I had been up for the past few nights, unable to sleep from all the nightmares and images that were stuck in my head. I was getting ready to bounce to get my hair done. Nessa had been able to squeeze me into her morning slot. As depressing as Jasmine's death was, I still had to move on. After all, Jasmine had become a problem for me and a big-ass headache to get rid of. She would have gotten dealt with one way or the other. That was what I had to keep telling myself. That was what I was thinking before a call came through on Rene's cell phone. The voice on the other end belonged to a man.

"Rene, honey, where are you?"

"Honey? Man, who the fuck is this?"

"I beg your pardon?"

"Who are you, and how do you know Rene?"

The man cleared his throat. "This is her fian—"

Click.

"Hello? Hello!" I looked at the screen and saw that I had lost the signal.

I hadn't been able to make out what he was trying to say. I redialed the number. This time a polite female voice answered.

"Thanks for calling First United Bank. Have you heard about our new CD rates?"

"Um, I'm just trying to find out who called me a while ago on my cell," I said.

"Okay, ma'am. May I get your name?"

I quickly shouted out Rene's name.

"Rene Brown," she repeated as she pecked away at her computer. "Okay, Miss Brown. I don't show any messages left for you from your banking officer, Vincent, so I'm sure it was just a routine customer courtesy call."

"All right," I said, pretending that I knew exactly what she was talking about.

"Was there anything else I could help you with, Miss Brown?"

"Yeah, sure. Can you tell me how much I have in my account?"

"Let's see here. I just need you to verify your most recent deposit."

I had no earthly idea. "I can't remember. I left my checkbook at home," I lied.

"Oh, I see. Well, if you can just verify your street address and the last four digits of your Social Security number, please."

I told her.

"Yes, ma'am, I do show that your balance as of today is ten thousand two hundred fifty-six dollars."

My jaw dropped, and all I could think was, *Oh shit.* I hung up from talking to the customer service rep, who had just given me some valuable information. Rene had plenty of money, and she was hiding it from me. Why was she being so secretive? We definitely needed to talk. I had to find Rene.

I didn't even have a chance to sit down good before my cell started ringing off the hook again. The message that appeared said unavailable.

Here we go again.

Rene

"Rene, are you all right? How you feelin'?"

My vision was blurred, and Shun looked like she had two heads and a swollen nose.

"Is she all right, Doc?"

"Yes, ma'am. She did fine back there. She's still under the anesthesia, but she's doing great," my doctor said to Shun as he reached for my hand.

"Okay, Mrs. Montgomery. I'm gonna let you get your rest now. I'll be back in a little while to check on you. If you need anything, let the nurses know." He turned to face Shun. "It's a good thing you brought her in when you did."

Dr. Isaga had on blue scrubs and a matching hair cover. He also looked much bigger to me than ever before. He patted me on my hand and walked out the door. I hated hospitals. I had never been admitted to one until now, but I knew already that I hated them. The smell, the colors, and most of all the newborn babies, whom I could hear crying down the hall. It was all depressing. I was clearly out of it because of the medicines they had drugged me with, but I could still recall the reason I was here.

"Shun," I called out in a raspy whisper.

"I'm here, baby. Just get some rest. Don't worry. I'm right here."

Everything in the room was still turning. I was dizzy, and the bright lights above my bed were blinding me and making my head hurt. I closed my eyes and hoped I wouldn't wake up. I wanted to be with Mariah, Mama's baby.

When I woke the next morning, I spotted Shun asleep in a chair, in an uncomfortable position. She was wearing the same thing from the night before. She had stayed overnight with me. That was a friend indeed. She was right there by my side, snoring. I looked around the small dimly lit room, noticing things that made tears pour out all over again. Someone had brought in a pink and yellow box and had placed it on the side table, next to a small lamp. I opened the box, and inside was a pink and blue baby blanket, a small brown teddy bear, and two Precious Moments sympathy cards. Each one started off with, "We are sorry for your loss. . . ." I couldn't read anymore. Tears were streaming down the sides of my face, and I felt like my heart was bleeding internally. I didn't realized that I was weeping so loudly. Shun woke up.

"What's wrong, baby?" She was wiping away the dried saliva that had formed around the corners of her mouth and down her chin.

"I'm okay," I lied. She could tell I wasn't.

She stood up and reached down to hug me. I cried; she cried; we cried together. She attempted to console me the best way she knew how. An hour later and I had finally gotten ahold of myself. Shun wanted to know what had happened. I spilled everything about the fight I had had and how we had been right all along about Sand cheating on me.

"I knew it!" Shun hollered. "She don't stay gone all day for nothing. You should have seen this coming, Rene. I told you she was no good. I just knew it."

I held my head down because I wasn't any better. I just hadn't got caught.

"See, I know what's good for you. You need a good man like Vincent."

"You're right. And that's exactly why I'm not going to tell him that I lost the baby."

"What do you mean, you're not going to tell him?"

"I'm saying that I need more time to process everything that has happened. He'll know in due time."

It was Saturday morning, about 10:17 a.m., according to my watch. I waited at the bus stop in front of Baylor University Medical Center for the next bus to come. I had just walked out without being discharged. As a matter of fact, I had overheard one of the other nurses say that my doctor was going to keep me there for another couple of days to run more tests. Shit, not if I could help it. As soon as she left my room to get another nurse to put my IV in, I'd made a run for it. I'd snatched off the gown, thrown on my clothes, and shot ghost.

I looked a hot mess in the red tank top and jogging pants I was admitted in, but guys were still blowing their horns and trying to give me curbside assistance. I thought the bus would never come. Public transportation sucked. It was nothing I could get used to. At least the weather was nice. The sun was beaming, but the wind was blowing a nice little breeze. It was perfect out. On days like this Sand and I would go to White Rock Lake to picnic. I would make sandwiches, and she would whip up a fruit basket. We would sit on our blanket, eat our sandwiches, and then she would feed me the strawberries, kiwi, and grapes one by one. After that she would play in my hair and read me poetry that she had written. Boy, how I missed those days. Now the thought of us ever being together was stomach turning. I could never be with her like that again.

The long yellow and black bus pulled up alongside the curb. It stopped right in front of the long pole with a sign that read DART. I hopped up, abandoning the comfortable Indian-style seating position I was in, and climbed on the bus. I paid my fare and walked toward the back, the same habit Sand had. Back when we were homeless, we would head to the back of the bus, and I would lean on her shoulder, fall asleep, and doze until we reached our destination. Those were again times when I had thought I knew myself, knew who I was, and what I was doing. Now I was up in church every Sunday, trying to redefine my life.

My relationship with Sand had cost me my first job. She thought that I had quit. Please, I would have never quit a job that was paying me fourteen an hour to do practically nothing. I had made good money, and the benefits had been great. The only complaint I had had was that my coworkers were backstabbing.

"May I help you with something?" That would be Rasheeka Jones. Rasheeka was a black woman in her midthirties. She was rude as hell, with no professionalism whatsoever.

"Good morning," I said once I noticed the receptionist, who had been too caught up in her phone conversation to have heard me walk through the door five minutes ago. She had magazines and catalogs of different sorts scattered across her desk. *Avon, Jet, Essence.* "Are you guys hiring for—"

"No, sorry. Not at this time."

She hadn't even let me complete my sentence. I figured the administrative position that I had seen in the newspaper was a misprint, or maybe I had the wrong firm. But Johnson and Johnson was the only black-owned and black-operated law firm that I knew of that was downtown.

"Yes, we are hiring, Rasheeka. Give this young lady an application." That was Theodore Wright, the company's vice president. "I'm running an ad in the *Dallas Morning News*." Theodore was sexy as hell. And that gold band around his finger meant he was also very married. He wore olive-green slacks with a black, long-sleeved, collared shirt and a matching tie and shoes. The type that preferred a bald head, manicured fingernails, and a clean-shaven face. He could have been Montel Williams's twin, only taller.

Rasheeka stood from her comfortable sitting position, having to put her reading materials to the side. "Girl, let me call you back," she said into the phone. She hung up the telephone and walked over to the filing cabinets behind her desk. She retrieved a manila folder. Rasheeka was a large woman, but she was pretty, with cocoa-butter skin. She had on a plum-colored dress and a black scarf. "Fill this out. And you must have a high school diploma or a GED, and we run a background and credit check before you are considered for candidacy."

I filled out the two-page application and walked it back to Rasheeka when I was done. She sat at her desk, polishing over the chipped coat of red on her nails. She looked over my entire application, not caring that she smeared red polish on the first page.

"Theodore," she hollered.

He came out of his office, which was right next to her little spot.

"She finished. What you want me to do with this?"

Theodore gave me an on-the-spot interview. I was hired in minutes.

It wasn't until I returned for the first day of work that I realized I had been hired to replace Rasheeka. I sat at her desk and in her same chair. Theodore had fired her rude ass. We didn't see each other again until she came in for her last paycheck.

Now, Mindy, a smart, young black college graduate who had the potential to become a great lawyer, was our intern. She was the one who helped train me for the job. I almost cried when Theodore told me that her boyfriend had committed suicide. She quit her job, and no one heard anything else from her after that.

Now the drama didn't really start until Theodore hired Philip. He was a temp. I knew from the moment he walked in the door that things were about to get wild. He was a shit starter. And I thought Shun gossiped. *Please.* She didn't have shit on him. He would go out of his way to find the scoop on everybody and then would dish the dirt out over lunch or via email correspondence. Philip was the missing-in-action CEO's sidekick. They were buddies. I didn't know if that was because Philip kept a handle on what went on when the big man wasn't in the office or what. But when I finally met Mr. Albery Johnson, I was flabbergasted. He was this short guy with a bad limp and a lazy eye. When talking to him, you weren't sure if he was looking directly at you or if he was looking around for something. The shit was some kind of scary.

And out of all the men to have ever had a secret crush on me, Albery was the most determined at making sure I knew it. He would walk over to my desk and chat about nothing. He had a wife, but that didn't stop him. I wanted to call her and tell her what a dog of a husband she had. He would leave tickets to games and jazz band concerts on my desk and would give me invites to dine with him at exotic restaurants that I couldn't even pronounce the names of. I politely turned down each and every invitation. Soon after, out of nowhere, a rumor started circulating that Theodore and I had something going on. It was a blatant lie, and I knew the one person who could have started it— Philip. One morning I went to work and

I spotted Theodore in his office, removing the frames and plaques from his wall.

"What's going on, Theodore? Why are you taking your pictures down?" I asked from the doorway to his office.

He was quiet for a moment. Then he told me that Albery had asked him to resign. If he didn't, he would be terminated. I couldn't believe it, but I knew the reason for this.

Albery still continued to hang out around the office and make passes at me. I wanted to yell sexual harassment, but I knew Albery could arrange it so that I never stepped foot in any office again. Albery had money, and money had power. I dealt with the harassment and the uncomfortable feelings that I had all while I worked there until one day Philip spotted Sand and me. We were in the parking lot, kissing and holding each other. I was sure that no one had seen me, but later on that day at work. Philip broadcast my business, and somehow it got back to Albery. He called me into his office and told me his company didn't need my services any longer. He told me he would get Janice, his pretty, young new assistant, to write me a letter of recommendation. I walked out but couldn't leave the building without getting some shit off my chest. I walked into the break room, where Philip loved to hang out. There were two other employees in there with him. He had a devilish grin across his face.

"Oh, Rene, how are you?" He started snickering, and I wanted to reach over and slap the shit out of him.

"You know what, Philip? You might as well be gay your damn self, the way you ride Albery's dick." Seeing the look on his face made me crack a smile.

"What? Who told you that? Tyrone is my roommate," he blurted, trying to sound convincing. Everyone was listening in, and he looked like he was about to cry.

I'd be damned. That muthafucka had the word *gay* written all over his damn face. I should have known.

Remembering that day and the sacrifices I had made for Sand was what I did the entire bus ride to the house. The apartment was about a block down. I pressed the button for the driver to stop at the next bus stop. He did. I hopped off and walked quickly through the apartments. When I saw Sand's car wasn't there, I made a run for it. I had left my purse home last night, so I had to use the spare key from underneath the rug in order to get in.

The house was a mess. Sand and her girlfriend must have been having a ball since I'd been gone, I figured. I ran in the bedroom, grabbed some clothes, and snatched up my purse. My cell phone was missing, and so was my key ring with my house and car keys. I didn't have time to search for them. I quickly wrote a letter and left it on the table, kissed my apartment good-bye, and bounced. I locked the door using my spare and paid June Bug across the street to nigga rig my car. He took an old key he had and shaped it to fit in the ignition. He had been a lock-smith and a professional car thief back in the day. I didn't know how in the hell he had got the maintenance position for the apartments with his record.

I knew a lot about him because Shun knew someone who had been locked down with him. When she saw him come over to the apartment one day to fix my dishwasher, she'd panicked.

"What he doing in here?" she'd whispered. "Girl, he gonna rob y'all asses blind. Watch and see. Oh, my God. Let me go before he snatch my wallet. Lord knows I only got about two dollars in it, anyway."

"Thanks, June. I owe you one," I said once my car's engine started.

"You already know what I want," he said, licking his crusty fat lips. He had had a crush on me since I moved in. He was a large dark-skinned brotha, but he was not my type. I had to hide from him sometimes, because I didn't want to have to keep telling him that I was already seeing someone, even though he saw Sand almost every day. I mean, hell, he lived directly across the parking lot from us.

"Nah, June. I can't help you out there. Sorry," I said.

And then I hurriedly drove away. I was gone forever. No looking back. Did somebody say, "Sand?" *Sand who? I ain't never heard of her.*

Vincent finally came to the door after I had banged on it long enough. It was late in the afternoon. He looked depressed, and more than that, he looked as if something was bothering him.

"Hey, babe," I said cheerfully. He cracked the door just halfway, forcing me to push it all the way open to keep from having to squeeze through.

"Hey," he shot back in a low, relaxed voice. "Why didn't you use your key?"

"Lost it," I said, although I was sure it was back at the house somewhere.

He walked back into the front room, where he had been stretched out on the sofa bed. I followed closely behind him.

"Where you been? I've been trying to call you all day on your cell phone." He lay back across the bed.

"With Shun, honey," I lied. It was a damn shame how lies seemed to roll off the tip of my tongue with hardly any effort. I was becoming a habitual liar. But my excuse was that I was lying for a good enough reason.

"She needed me to watch the kids for her these past couple of days, while she went job hunting," I continued. "You know that Jo Jo is the only one in school, and she can't afford to send the other three to day care or pay for a babysitter. So I help her out sometimes."

I was just lying my black ass off, knowing damn well Shun had them kids in day care and she wasn't at all out of pocket. The government was paying for it. She dropped them off at six in the morning and didn't pick them up until the place closed.

He turned to face me, looking oddly expressionless, as if he was trying to read me. His left hand rested under his chin as he stared me down.

"They called about your grandma," he said.

"What!" The spit I had just swallowed was almost my cause of death. I choked so badly that the clamp holding my ponytail in place flew off and my watering eyes could have been mistaken for tear-filled ones. I looked up at him after catching my breath. "Who called?"

"The nursing home."

I almost peed my pants. I was already tripping over words, and now I couldn't think of shit to say. I continued to stand there in astonishment, feeling bewildered, trying not to give myself away with my reactions.

"How come you didn't tell me you were going to put her in a nursing home, after all? You sly thing, you. I knew you would see it my way sooner or later. It was best," he said, smiling and rising up from the mattress.

I hadn't blinked once. I was still standing there, in shock. I wanted to ask more questions. I wanted to drill him and ask who, what, when, where, but I didn't. I had to follow along.

"Yeah, honey. I forgot to mention that. I was saving it for a surprise. I was going to tell you over dinner. I also have some more exciting news."

"What?" He was still looking deep into my eyes, not letting the eye contact break.

"I was talking to a wedding coordinator, and she suggested that we do a fall wedding. I told her the baby was due in April, I mean, is due in April, and she said that if you wanted to be married before it got here, then we should do it now, while there aren't many fall weddings already booked. I was thinking this month."

"You want to get married this month?" He looked at me like he had a hard time hearing.

"Sure. I think it'll be better. Like you said, let's do it before the baby gets here." I was flipping shit around every which way. "I actually think it's a terrific idea, because when Mariah gets here, I will already be Mrs. Rene Montgomery." I flashed a smile and waved my ring at him.

Vincent was still looking at me funny, but I guessed he was just admiring me like always. "Well, if you've thought this over, and that's what you want, let's do it." He smiled, then leaned in to kiss me on the cheek.

In the meantime, I was trippin' over who could have called. All of a sudden my imaginary grandma had become real. That was a measly problem for the time being. It could have just been a coincidence, and if indeed it was, it was perfect timing. I still had to play it safe, though, just in case. I hopped on the Internet and typed in "Ways to get pregnant fast." I jotted down all the sex positions, the foods that were recommended, the home remedies, and a list of fertility drugs that were highly ranked to speed up the process. I had to get pregnant quick. Vincent was in for the ride of his life. Remedy number one: the more sex, the better the chances. *Fuck, fuck, fuck.*

Sand

"Hello."

"I know you're sleeping with my girlfriend. I've seen the both of you in clear view. Her legs wrapped around your head, you two kissing and slobbering on each other. I can't stand women like you. It's disgusting." *Click.*

The caller disconnected the call. I couldn't tell if the voice on the other end had belonged to a male or a female. The caller had whispered the entire call. I had no idea who it could have been. Jasmine was the only female I had fucked with that could have possibly been involved with anyone. I didn't understand how somehow, someway, she still managed to cause chaos in my life.

I looked around the house, and suddenly the loneliness and the emptiness that I was feeling reminded me that I was missing the hell out of Rene. It had been three days since I slept next to her. I couldn't stand it. The cucumber smell coming from the plug-ins that she had in every electrical outlet reminded me even more of her.

I went into the kitchen and fixed a bowl of Honey Nut Cheerios. I sat on the couch, ate, and watched a rerun of the show *Martin*. Pam and Martin were going at it, like always. I found myself laughing out loud.

My mind started wandering off. I thought about my deceased mother and my father, who I had not seen in years. I wondered how my pops was doing and if he thought about me as often as I thought about him. I wondered if my aunt Maba was still sick with diabetes and if my uncle Robbie, my dad's youngest brother, was up in heaven with my mother. I had heard from one of my cousins whom I had bumped into at the mall that he had passed a few months before my mom did. My cousin Jimmy had told me that Robbie suffered from the "gay man's disease." I knew he was talking about AIDS. I really missed my family, and at that moment I was missing my girl. I watched television until nothing was on except for infomercials. My eyes began to get heavier as I tried to fight off sleep. I took a few more hits of the Black & Mild cigar I had lit up and then slowly drifted off on the couch.

The following day I sat in Nessa's chair, getting my hair braided for opening night. She was braiding and chatting with a friend at the same time.

"Sand, I'd like you to meet my friend Deja."

I straightened my posture after being slouched down in the same position for so long. It was going on two hours, and Nessa was still braiding my hair. She'd said she was going to do something that nobody had ever had. My ass was cramped up, and my legs had fallen asleep on me. My ass was hurtin', and I had to pee, but the single bathroom stall was out of service, so I had no choice but to hold it.

I hadn't seen Deja walk in, because I was nodding off to sleep, but I knew that if I had, I would have been hawking. Nessa turned my chair around so that I came face-to-face with a statue of beauty. Deja was about five feet seven and 150 pounds. She was one of those smooth-skinned, Hershey's chocolate sisters. She had almond-shaped dark brown eyes, thick curled lashes, and perfectly arched eyebrows. She even had deep dimples like Rene. Ooh, shit, and those lips were screaming my name. Not too big and not too small, they were perfectly designed for kissing. Her makeup was light and natural, with an added touch of lip gloss to accent those luscious lips. She eyed me as she extended her hand.

"Sand, Deja's gonna come with me tonight to check out your new club."

Deja can go anywhere she pleases, I thought to myself. But I didn't have to think this; my facial expression and my body gestures gave me away. Deja was bangin'. I bit down on my bottom lip and stroked my invisible beard. My hand met hers. Hers was softer, smoother than mine. I wanted to just kiss each fingertip and caress her hand with my tongue.

"How you doing, Mrs. Deja?" I said. I hoped Nessa still had a long way to go on my hair, because suddenly, I had all the time in the world.

"Oh, I'm not a Mrs.," she said, correcting me. She smiled, affording me a beautiful view of her pearly whites. I could definitely picture her on a Colgate tooth-paste commercial.

"I apologize," I said. "I was just sure that a nice young man had already scooped you up and taken you off the market."

She looked at Nessa and burst into laughter.

"What? Did I say something wrong?" I was looking at both of them, trying to figure out what it was that I had said that was so funny.

Nessa kind of shook her head. I looked back at Deja. She flicked her tongue at me, and there it was, a rain-bow-colored tongue ring. So she was family, and a reunion for me it was about to be. Before I could go any further, she felt the need to enlighten me about a few things.

"I fuck with women, but femmes only. I don't do studs. It defeats the purpose of being with a woman."

"Aw, shit," I heard Nessa say, predicting the conversa-tion was headed for a sharp turn.

"What do you mean, it defeats the purpose?" I asked in self-defense, as well as out of curiosity. I sat up a little straighter and folded my hands in my lap, waiting for her to tell me.

"It just does, for me, anyway. I don't see myself ever being with a man again, so why would I want a woman who dressed like one to remind me of that? I mean, if you have to pretend to be something you're not just to get a woman's attention, then evidently you're confused about your own identity."

I sat still, listening to Deja, who was even sexier when she spoke. Luckily, there were no guys around, because if there had been, we wouldn't have been able to carry on this heated discussion.

"Oh, hell. She about to go deep on you, Sand," Nessa said jokingly, cautioning me before I could dig myself into a deeper hole.

"Well, Mama, I can understand where you comin' from, but I really don't agree with that. Have you ever tried looking at it from another angle?"

"What you mean, another angle? I don't look at the sideshows. I watch the main event," Deja replied.

Nessa started laughing. "I told you, Sand. Don't do it. She'll skin you alive."

I shifted my position in my seat. "I'm saying, have you ever looked at it another way? Like in someone else's shoes?"

"No, I haven't had to."

"Has it crossed your mind that if someone was born a woman but dressed like a man, they did it because that's the way they viewed themselves? I mean, I can see how you could have formed your opinion on the matter, but not all studs view themselves as women trying to be men. Some of us feel like we are men trapped in women's bodies."

Deja sat down in one of the nearby barber chairs. She was still facing me, and I had not removed my eyes from her. She had me caught up in her love spell.

Nessa was just tuning in and braiding at the same time so she could be finished before her other scheduled clients arrived.

"So, are you telling me"—Deja took a breath—"that you feel like a man trapped in a woman's body?"

I normally didn't discuss my personal life with a stranger, but this was an exception. Somebody had to open baby girl's mind up a little bit more, and I just felt that me being the one could be considered a privilege.

"Yes, that's exactly what I'm saying."

She stood up, walked over to the vending machine, and retrieved a Diet Dr Pepper. "So you believe it's something like a birth defect?"

"If that's the way you wanna put it, yeah."

She sat back down in the chair and took a sip of her soda. "Hmm," she said, jerking her head back, pondering all she had just been told. "That's something . . . a birth defect. I never looked at it like that."

I suddenly remembered that I was pressed for time. I had a grand opening to get ready for. "Well, you can't be in the game and not know everyone's position," I said and winked.

She looked at me crazily. "I thought I needed only to know mine."

"No, ma'am. Not when you're on the same team," I replied.

She suddenly got quiet, and all you could hear was the boom box Nessa had on, which was playing one of Keyshia Cole's latest hits. "I should've cheated. . . ," the singer lamented.

"All finished," Nessa said, turning me back around in the chair so that I faced the wall mirror. I loved the style before I could even see it all the way. She had hooked me up. She had done small-sectioned zigzag braids at the top, Iversons on the sides, and straight braids at the back, with black and green beads dangling from the ends to match the hunter-green and black camouflage pants and black muscle tee I wore. She'd sprayed me down with oil sheen. I had the diamond studs in my ears that Rene had gotten me for graduation, and they were shining. The reflection in the mirror was gleaming in Deja's face.

"Damn, this is tight." I used the handheld mirror to check out the back.

"I know this." Nessa laughed, pointing to herself. "I'm that bad bitch." She sang along with the song that was now playing on the radio. I thought the cat's name was Webbie.

I peeled off a fresh and crisp big face. "Will this do it?" I asked, handing her the one-hundred-dollar bill.

"Fo' sho." She tucked the bill into her bra, as usual.

"I'ma see you tonight, right?" I asked her.

She stood behind me and removed the cape. "Yes, Nessa will be in the house. I already worked out my arrangements with my baby daddy, so I will be there, getting loose."

"Uh, not getting loose," I teased.

"Yes, loose, baby. Like this." Nessa danced to the music, rotating her butt and backin' it up. She was crazy.

Deja walked up to me. "Nessa, I like that." She was looking me over, and even though she was behind me, checking out the artwork on the back, I could feel her eyes in other places. "So, who's Rene?" She was now looking at the beautiful woman whose face was tatted on my upper left arm, with "Rene" written below it.

"My girlfriend," I answered proudly.

"She's pretty."

"Thank you. Well, I gotta be going, Nessa."

Nessa was sweeping the floor, picking up the hair she had clipped off. It looked like a chunk, but my shit was still down to my shoulders.

"Come on, Deja, so I can bump your hair," Nessa said.

Deja brushed past me and flopped down in the seat that I had warmed up. "Sand, I want you to know that I heard everything you were saying earlier. No hard feelings, right?"

"Oh, none at all."

Deja showed me that Colgate smile again.

I smiled back. "See you sexy ladies tonight," I said, and then I headed out the front door. I had to get back on schedule. I had a lot of shit I needed to do before nightfall.

Today was the big day. So far everything was working out according to plan, and even the weather was in my favor. I rode down the streets of Pleasant Grove, heading home. I needed to make some calls and drop some clothes off at Smith's.

I pulled up to the apartments and Rene's car was not parked in the usual spot. It was gone. The apartment felt empty the instant I stepped inside. There was a note on the dining room table. It was from Rene. I picked it up and began to read.

To Sand:

How could you? I thought I meant everything to you. How could you do me like this? As much as it hurts me to write this, I realize now this letter was long overdue. All these years, all these years, Sand, I thought we knew each other. Knew what each other wanted and desired. Evidently, we both were wrong.

I let you raise me into something that I'm not and would never be, but because I loved you, I couldn't leave. I loved you as a person and for who you were inside, but you took advantage of my vulnerability and kindness. My mistake was that I didn't recognize it in the very beginning. I opened up to you. I shared everything with you. And as much as I pretended along with you to be what I knew all along I wasn't, you still managed to hurt me. You were a selfish lover at that, while I shared my inner soul.

Well, it's too late now. I knew there was something missing in our relationship all along. Trust. I found myself someone new. Yes, Sand, someone that I can share lovemaking with, instead of feeling like a damn kitchen appliance that only gets used when someone needs a quick fix.

That's all I have to say. Have a good life, and thank you for making my transition into my new life so much easier. Good-bye . . . forever.

Rene

P.S. I met her. I hope you two are happy together.

Sand

What did she mean, her transition into her new life? And what she mean when she said she felt like a kitchen appliance? She was truly trying to crush me, and her mission was almost accomplished. Rene needed to know that I had never loved any other woman except for her. She was all I needed. I had fucked up. I admitted it. That was a mistake. I had known that eventually the shit would come back around on me some kind of way. I had known that I would not get off scot-free. I could fess up to my mistake. If I could only talk to Rene, I'd admit to all the wrong shit that I had ever done. I couldn't let her leave me like this.

I began to feel a void in my heart just from reading the letter she had written. The words began to sink in more. She had hit me hard, and it hurt like hell. I balled up the piece of paper and chucked it in the trash. I headed to the bedroom and checked the drawers. Most of her things were gone. I checked the bathroom. Her toothbrush, makeup bags, and perfumes, which were normally on the counter, were also gone. Rene had left me.

I knew she had to be at Shun's house. I searched the caller ID on Rene's phone. There were no phone numbers that I recognized off the bat. If I knew Rene like I thought I did, her homegirl would have been the first person she called before she walked out the door, especially since I had her cell phone. That was, if Shun hadn't been here with her, helping her pack up her shit. I took my chances and hit the redial button on the receiver, hoping it would direct me to where she was. A little boy answered after the third ring. It was Jo Jo, Shun's oldest boy.

"Is Rene there?" I asked as soon as he said hello. I could hear loud noises in the background.

"My aunt Rene not here."

I could hear Shun's big-ass mouth also, hollering over the television. "Jo Jo, who that on the phone!"

"My mama said, 'Who calling?'"

"Tell her to come to the phone, li'l man."

"Mama, somebody want you. They said to come to the phone."

I could hear Shun's voice getting closer and closer. "Clean up this damn house and get y'all's black asses off that damn video game before I throw it in the trash. It don't make no sense, my house looking like this! Hello."

I had had to give it my all even to call her; now I was going to have to really put my pride to the side and actually speak to the woman.

"How you doing, Shun?"

"Well, well, well, if it ain't Cassandra. It is either snowing outside or Dallas is about to get an earthquake, because I know you misdialed."

"Actually, Shun, I'm looking for Rene."

"Oh, so you call me, figuring that I would know where she is? No, wait. Figuring I'd tell you where she is?"

"Shun, really all I need you to do is tell me if you know where she might be. I have to talk to her. She came home, and she left me a note. I need to explain some things to her. I need to talk to her." I was desperate.

She started laughing. "Okay, so now you're feeling bad about her finding out about your little girlfriend?"

"Girlfriend? What girlfriend?"

"Your little secret booty call you've been running to when you leave her alone."

"What did she tell you?"

"Nuh-uh. I will not betray my friend like you did. I'm just glad she left your ass before Vincent found out."

I paused and had to rewind what she'd said. "What you mean, before Vincent found out? Who the fuck is Vincent?" I tried to keep from yankin' her ass through the telephone. Shun was fuckin' with me now. Yeah, this bitch was really fuckin' with me big-time.

"Her boyfriend, Vincent, the one she was . . . Wait a minute. She didn't tell you?"

"Tell me what?" I hollered into the phone.

"That she was leaving you for Vincent? She called me and told me she had told you everything."

Man, this shit was giving me a headache, and I didn't know whether I wanted to punch a hole in the wall or scream into one of the throw pillows over on the love seat. I just knew my body temperature was starting to rise.

"Forget I said anything. I'm busy. I gotta go." Shun hung the phone up in my face, leaving me with the dial tone. I actually held that receiver in my hand long enough for the operator to come on.

Something wasn't adding up. I tried calling back, but she must have taken the phone off the hook, because all I kept getting was a busy signal. *That bitch*. Shun was really starting to piss me off, but she knew something I didn't. I needed to find Rene, and I needed to find her now.

I left the apartment and walked down the stairs and over to my car, which was parked right in front of the building, in Rene's usual spot. There was a black Lincoln Navigator alongside my ride. I had never seen this SUV before and I knew no one in my building owned it. I pulled my keys out of my pocket. I needed to ride around a few minutes and blow off some steam before I did something crazy. If Rene was cheating on me, then I had to be ready to catch a murder case. Somebody was gon' die. Rene was mine.

I mashed my cigar into the concrete after inhaling a few more puffs. I heard the passenger-side window go down on the Nav, and the guy in the vehicle tried to get my attention.

"Excuse me, sir." He climbed out of his luxurious Lincoln and walked over to where I was standing.

"What's up?" I asked. He looked like an undercover lawman. I would break before I let him take me to jail. He checked me out, scoping me up and down, and looked around as if he was lost. "Can I help you with something, man?"

Nah, he couldn't be no law; he looked too damn scary. But this white boy was bold as hell to be bringing his ass over here to the hood. He was asking to get that black beauty of his repossessed, courtesy of the neighborhood gangbangers. That would make a real nice ride to roll around in on a Saturday night. This dude had some manufactured rims and a leather interior, and the Nav was waxed down, looking like it had just rolled off the showroom floor.

"I'm not from around here, and I believe I may be lost. You see, I'm looking for a friend of mine who I haven't seen in a long, long time. And I looked through the phone book, and I found an address for her here in these apartments, but I'm having trouble locating the correct building that she might live in. I'm trying to deliver to her the news that her parents are in town and they're staying at my place. They've been looking for her. Do you by chance happen to know anybody by the name of Rene Brown?"

"Rene Brown?" I repeated. "Yeah, I know her quite well. She lives right here in the same building as me."

"Oh, thank God. Her parents and I have been searching all over Dallas, looking for that girl. You won't believe how happy they'll be when I tell them I found their daughter."

I reached my hand out to him. "I'm Sand," I said. "Rene's girlfriend." His eyebrows rose as he offered his hand and then exchanged a firm, manly handshake.

"How interesting." He folded his arms and smiled.

"I'm not sure where she's at right now. I was just about to go see if I could catch up with her at one of her hangouts."

"Oh, I wish I could come with you and be there when you tell her that her parents are in town. They haven't seen each other in years."

I looked him over once again. I was also ready to share the news that Rene's parents were looking for her. She had never really talked much about them, besides saying that she had ended up in a foster home when she was younger because neither one of them had wanted her. Since I knew very little about Rene's past, I saw this as an opportunity to get as much information as I could out of this dude.

"You can roll if you want. Ain't no problem. She can't be that far. She normally runs at the track around the corner. We can try there first."

He hit the automatic switch for his car alarm, and you could hear the locks lock into place, setting his alarm.

"Before we go, do you mind if I have something to drink? I'll take water. I'm parched from riding around, looking for Rene all night."

"Sure, my man. Come on up with me." I led him up the steps and into the apartment. His hands were in his pockets, and he looked paranoid as fuck. I was laughing inside. I walked over to the kitchen bar and grabbed a glass on the little stand Rene had there.

"That's a nice picture there." He walked over to the fireplace, where a huge framed picture of Rene and me hung. "Boy, look at her. She hasn't changed a bit, except for growing a little more in other departments." He grinned.

"Yeah, she all woman now," I commented, also looking up at the picture. In it we both were standing, with me behind her, my arms relaxed around her waist. I wished that moment could have lasted forever. Me holding her, touching her. I wished I could be that close to her now.

Dude's eyes roamed all over our living room. "This a nice place you guys got here."

"'Preciate it!" I called out from the kitchen. "My man, I have some fresh lemonade and tea in here." Rene loved to make fresh lemonade and sweet tea.

"Tea will do just fine!"

I poured him a glass and took it to him.

He took a sip. "Um, this tastes so familiar." He smiled, then finished the drink.

White boy had taste for real. It looked like he had a thing for black women too, because when we passed my two neighbors while heading back down the stairs to my car, I caught him looking at their asses. *Blue-eyed devil*. I spotted June Bug across the street, staring me down, as usual. I pretended I didn't see his nosy ass.

When we reached the bottom step, I looked up and there was a fine-ass female walking toward me. She was picking up the pace.

"Sand," I heard her holler.

She was practically sprinting toward me. As she grew closer, I knew exactly who she was. She pulled the shades down from her face, and the first thing I saw was a black eye. There was also a deep cut across the left side of her face, near her eye.

"Damn, baby girl, what the hell happened to you?" I said.

She looked over at the white man standing at my side.

"Nope, it ain't even like that," I assured her before any thoughts ran across her mind. "This here is my boy . . ."

"Oh, I'm Michael, but call me Mike."

"Mike," I repeated after him.

"Sand, I really need to talk to you."

"Come on, Peaches. Can it wait? Me and Mike gotta go handle up on somethin'."

"No. I need to talk to you now." Her voice was very demanding, and she had a look in her eyes that was really scary.

"Yeah, all right." I looked up at Mike. "Let me see what's up, man. It'll only take a few."

"Oh, go ahead. I have nowhere else to devote my time." He walked over to his ride and hopped inside.

"Now, what's up, Mama?"

Teardrops started rolling down her cheeks. "Sand, you gotta get outta here."

"What! What are you talking about?"

"They gonna kill you."

"What? Who?"

I grabbed her hands and pulled them away from her face so that I could look into her eyes. She was obviously bothered and embarrassed about the black eye and the cut that had threatened her beautiful face. She looked at me sadly.

"Have you been watching the news? Did you see what they did to Jasmine?" she asked. She started crying even more. I had to grab her and pull her up. She leaned on my shoulders.

"Jasmine?" I said. "Who did what to Jasmine?" I didn't know if I should pretend I knew nothing about what had happened to Jasmine or if I should just pour out everything I had witnessed with my own two eyes the night I went over to her place. "What happened, Peaches? Talk to me."

I could barely understand anything she was saying through all the sobs and sniffles. "They killed her."

"Who killed her?"

"They knew you would go over there. Somehow they made it the perfect setup. They have your prints and everything on the doorknob and all over the place. They've been plotting this from day one."

"Who!" I practically yelled. Peaches kept taking me in circles. She wasn't giving me enough information to work with. "Who, Peaches?" I asked more calmly.

"James and Chyna."

I dropped my hands from her shoulders and backed up against the wall. *It can't be. This bitch is lying*, I thought. *There's no way. Not James. And why would Chyna want to fuck with me? We had no beef, as far as I knew. Something's not adding up.*

Peaches was still in front of me, crying. "What happened to your eye?" I asked her.

She held her head down. "I got into a fight with your girlfriend."

"You what!" I walked closer to Peaches. I wanted to strangle her if she hurt Rene.

Before I could say anything more, she said, "I came over here to tell you about all this mess you're in, and she wanted to fight. Sand, she hit me first. I wouldn't have touched your girl."

"So, this is why Rene up and left me. You're the reason she fuckin' left me?"

Before I knew it, my hands were gripping Peaches's throat. Mike jumped out of his car and had to pull me off of her.

"Calm down. Calm down." He had me in a lock where I couldn't even get my hands around him to go back at her.

I was gon' hurt her. Rene had left me, and Peaches was the reason why.

"I'm cool, dude," I told Mike. "I'm cool."

He eased up his grip and eventually let me go. Peaches flinched every time she saw me make a move.

"Sand, I'm sorry." She continued to cry.

"Man, how do you know all this shit?" I asked. Mike was standing next to me, making sure I didn't have another chance at ripping her face off. He stood there listening.

"Remember that night at your graduation party?"

"What about it?" I looked at her as if to say, "Keep talking and don't ask me no muthafuckin' questions."

"Remember how we ended up making love in the guest bedroom? You, me, and Jasmine."

I saw Mike turn his head in the opposite direction. I squinted my eyes at her, hinting that she could at least spare brother man the damn details.

"Well, we weren't alone that night," she revealed.

"What the fuck you mean?"

Mike turned his head back around.

"James paid me to go in that room and fuck you. I had no idea that Jasmine was even in there. I was giving some stinky-breath dude a table dance, and that's when James pulled me to the side and handed me two thousand dollars to go in there and have sex with you. I thought it was just a graduation gift or something. That was until I overheard James and Chyna talking."

I listened intently, replaying that night in my head. I remembered being fucked up. I remembered Jasmine arguing with somebody on her cell phone. After that, I remembered her walking me into the guest room.

"They were saying something about having you on tape with Jasmine and me. Then I overheard them saying they had to use you in order to get some girl to cooperate with

Chyna. Chyna said if she had to pay somebody to finish it off, she would, but she'd rather have this girl do the job for her to keep everything from getting messy. She said she had people that were ready to get paid, but she wanted—"

"Whoa," I said, interrupting her.

"And that's when I heard that Jasmine was dead."

"Whoa, whoa," I said, cutting her off. Mike was still listening in. This was too much information for him. "My man, I gotta handle some urgent business. Is it okay if I call you after I've found her and let you give her the news?"

"Sure. No problem. I have a better idea. When you handle everything you need to handle, why don't you come over and meet the folks yourself?"

"That sounds like a cool idea." I did want to meet Rene's parents. I wanted to see where she had got all her good looks. I also wanted to see the mother and father who were the reason for all her built-up anger and pain.

He slid me a piece of paper with his phone number, and underneath it, he wrote "Cell." He also jotted down his address. He hopped in his ride and took off. Mike was a cool dude, but I had forgot to ask him where he knew Rene from. I was real curious, because Rene had failed to mention having any male friends from the past.

"Something about that dude ain't right. Why the hell he actin' all nervous?" Peaches said.

"Mind your business, Peaches, and finish telling me." I watched Peaches closely. If I was the one who was gonna get killed, then why in the hell had her ass come running up here earlier, crying and shit like it was her ass on the line? Something wasn't sticking. I just couldn't trust a hooker. I had to find out the shit for myself, even if that meant going to James's house to talk.

I glanced at my cell. It was about ten minutes to five.

"Look, Peaches, thanks for looking out, but I gotta be going."

"Where are you going?"

"Thanks for the heads-up, but I have a club to be getting ready to open tonight." I headed for my ride. She walked back to the visitors' parking section and hopped in her little car.

I was on the highway before long, heading for James's place. I hoped that there wasn't any truth to what Peaches had just told me. I hoped that she had made the shit up. But why would she?

I placed the car in park when I reached James's place. James's Cadillac DeVille was nowhere in sight. I made sure there was no one around before I eased my way through the patio sliding glass door, which I knew he always left unlocked. I was looking for anything that I could find that would make Peaches's accusations legit.

I headed for the guest bedroom. Once inside, I noticed that the sheets that I remembered being on the bed had been changed. Now they were silver. Other than that, the entire room looked the same. Mirrors were on the ceiling right over the bed, capturing everything and anything. A silver champagne bucket was on the nightstand, with empty bottles of champagne, which I assumed were there just for decoration. I kept looking around, scanning the room, until I spotted something that was unusual. Directly across from me was an artificial plant near the bathroom. I walked over toward it, and there was a flashing red beam coming from it that caught my eye. I lifted one of the leaves and saw that it was actually covering a mini camcorder. I looked at the top of it. It was on pause. Peaches had told the truth. They were setting me up.

I ran out of the condo as quick as I could. I climbed in my ride and sped down I-75 all the way back home. My cell started ringing, and the caller ID read private.

"Hello?"

"Bitch, you're gonna die tonight."

I threw the phone out the window as hard as I could. I looked at the radio clock. It was 5:45 p.m. I looked at Rene's cell, which I had on the left side of my hip. It also read 5:45 p.m. I pushed my foot down a little more on the accelerator, pushing Ms. Lady to her max. I didn't give a damn about a ticket. I had to get home.

I walked through the door, out of breath. I grabbed a couple of bags out of the kitchen cabinet and went into the bedroom, then grabbed the only suitcase I owned out of the closet. I folded up shirts, pants, shorts and threw them in the suitcase, along with some boxers. I looked in my sock drawer, grabbed my stash of cash, and left.

I checked in at the nearby Motel 6. They put me in a nice comfy room. That was all I needed, at least until Monday. If Peaches was right about them having my prints, then that meant I was gonna go down for Jasmine's murder. But why in the hell would they have recorded me and Jasmine having sex? It just didn't sit right. Hell no. I had to get me a lawyer and get this shit corrected ASAP.

I counted my money. I had only about a grand. That wasn't shit. I needed to get to Rene quick. I needed her now. I knew I was in some deep shit. I could feel it. I didn't know how I was going to be able to function tonight at the club. I was being set up for some shit I didn't do, and somebody was after me, trying to kill me. I needed some protection fast, and I knew just where to get some.

Before I could count to three, I was back in the Grove. I went to a well-known pawnshop and purchased a nine-millimeter. The Arabian man watched me as I stared at it, almost too scared even to hold it.

"I give you a real good price on this one," he said, smiling. His buttery-yellow, rotten teeth were the first thing to catch my eye. I turned my focus from his yucky mouth, which desperately needed a dentist's appointment, back to the pistol. I admired the cold chrome-plated metal as it lay flat in the palm of my hand.

I gazed it, looked up at the man, who was hoping to make a sale, and said, "I'll take it."

Sand, what are you about to do? I stood there thinking, contemplating the damage one little bullet could do.

Rene

I jumped when I heard the door screech. Vincent peeked inside the small office, where I had been on the computer. I was still on the Internet, looking up some things. I tried to be as quiet as possible.

"Rene, I have some errands to run. Are you going to be here when I get back?"

I minimized the screen that showed all the sex positions that could increase my chances of conception and quickly brought up the screen with the baby beds and car seats. I turned around to face Vincent. "Yeah, honey, I'll be here. I'm all yours now."

He gave me a devilish grin and walked out the door, then shut it like it had been before he entered. I could hear the garage door opening and him reversing the car. Then I heard nothing. He was gone.

I pulled the first screen back up and started taking notes on the yellow notepad I had found underneath the computer. After I was satisfied with all the information I had gathered, I signed off and went into the living room. It was about twelve in the afternoon. I picked up the remote and switched the television station to channel four and was terrified at the disturbing images that appeared on the screen. Network 4's Brian Cage was reporting live at the scene of a crime.

"Yes, folks, this is by far the most horrific crime committed here in this neighborhood. Investigators are trying to piece together this bazaar attack that occurred here in this Fort Worth townhome. Here with us is Laura Shelton, a neighbor of the young victim, whose body was discovered only hours ago. Ma'am, do you mind telling us what you witnessed here today?"

The elderly woman seemed to be shaken up by everything. She placed her hand over her chest and started describing the way she had found the victim. "She was gone. I smelled this awful smell all the way into my house. I went over to check on Jasmine, but I didn't see nobody. The door was halfway open, so I let myself on through. I went to the back, and I saw her there . . . dead. She was gone." She began to get choked up. "Wasn't nothing I could do for her," she said, crying. "Poor child. She was only nineteen."

The camera went back to the reporter, who was talking and pointing in the direction of the crime scene. Yellow tape was all around the place, blocking off the spectators, who were as curious to know what had happened as I was. Some of them even had their babies wrapped in their arms. Younger children were running around, all trying to get on live television. You could see two men walking out of the house, carrying the dead body in a black body bag. People were screaming and hollering. I was not sure if they were screaming because they knew the young lady or if they were screaming because of the sight of the body bag.

"As you can see, this has affected the community greatly. We'll keep you updated as we learn more. Keep it tuned to Network Four. Back to you, Shannon."

That was crazy. I recognized those townhomes. They were about thirty minutes away from where my apartment was. *Wait a minute.* I didn't live there anymore. That was now Sand's place. I had my new home, and it was here with Vincent.

I straightened the living area and washed the few dishes that were left in the sink. Vincent was no housekeeper; that was for sure. I took in a great amount of air and sighed at the thought of what I had to look forward to in the near future. After straightening and cleaning, I decided to check on Shun and see if she had heard about what had happened over in the Emerald Terrace Townhomes.

"Hey, Jo Jo. Let me talk to your mama."

"Hey, Aunt Rene. She not here."

"Well, tell her that I called, and to call me back at my new place. She knows the number."

"All right."

As I hung up the phone, I felt great about myself. I felt that I had a burden totally removed from my shoulders. I was rid of Sand, and now things could be the way they were supposed to be.

I removed my belongings from the bag that I had brought in with me earlier. I folded my things neatly and placed them to the side, to be put in a drawer as soon as I could free up some space. I had also brought my stash along. Yes, my new best friends were gonna have to join me in my new place of residence. I couldn't leave them alone to be forgotten about. Nah, I just couldn't do that. That would be so cruel of me. I had given each one of them nicknames. I had the porno, which I now called Tease, and the vibrator, which I had given the name Rock Me. I placed Tease and Rock Me in the hall closet, on the top shelf. I was feeling the wifey thing already, and I hadn't even said, "I do," or jumped across the straw broom. I knew I was making the right decision; I just wished I had made it a lot sooner.

I'd been saving for this day for as long as I could remember. I had close to ten thousand dollars in the bank now. I had been saving up ever since the first paycheck I received from Johnson and Johnson. Sand had paid all the bills, so my checks had been basically all mine. On top of that, she had broken me off daily. I was no dumb broad. I had stacked my money for a rainy day, and that day was here. I would use most of it to give me a head start in my new life.

Vincent had said he had errands to run. That would give me enough time to shower, start dinner, and iron his clothes for the workweek to come. Yes, I could definitely do this. I started dinner first. I whipped up some pot roast, scalloped potatoes, green beans, and dinner rolls. I made some fresh squeezed lemonade and baked some homemade brownies for dessert.

When that was all finished, I hopped in the shower. I lathered my body up real nice and good, making sure to focus on those spots that I was going to steer Vincent to tonight. Unlike Sand, he had a problem eating pussy. I had never said anything to him about it, because I didn't want him to think that was all I was about. But tonight was the night that I would allow him to devour my sweetness. I was sweeter than maple syrup and as appetizing as a delicacy.

I switched the water temperature from warm to cool. Just thinking about the things I wanted Vincent to do and the way I wanted him to do them made me get moist between my legs. I slid my fingers down to see if the moisture was coming from the cool water that flowed down my spine to my ass or if it was my own self-made juices. It as indeed from me. I lowered my hand, brushed it swiftly up my inner thigh. *Ooh*, that sent a nice little tingle through me. I did it again. I received the same reaction. I had found what I believed to be the *hot spot*. I halted when I reached my split. I removed the detachable showerhead, which could also be used as a massager, to finish off what I had started.

My pussy lips were throbbing now more than before, and I was turned on by my own sexual explorations. I held the running showerhead in my left hand, freeing my right hand to participate in other exploratory studies. My right hand swept across my left breast and then across my right. I used it to bring my right nipple up to my lips. I used my tongue as a weapon that forced my nipples to surrender. They both were at full attention and longing for something long, big, and hard to glide over them. I closed my eyes to see if I could paint a vivid picture of Vincent fucking me, having it his way. I could not. The only picture I could paint was of me and Sand, and then of the white girl and the white boy who had hard-core sex in Tease. I couldn't even envision Vincent doing anything out of the ordinary, anything other than the missionary position he and I had assumed when I came over to visit. I hoped like hell that that was not all I had to look forward to in our marriage.

I kept my eyes closed, and even though I couldn't recall a time when Vincent and I had fucked each other's hearts out, I was gonna make believe that he had. I spread my legs open even more for Vincent, who was now below me, feasting in my love bowl. I let out a loud moan as the tip of his tongue did jumping jacks on my clit. I squeezed my ass cheeks together, because the tension was so strong that I was bound to explode. After his acrobatic mouth was finished there, he started up the center of my left thigh. He worked his way up until he was at my navel. I flung my head back and allowed my hair to tickle my shoulders and spine, adding to our foreplay.

His left hand massaged my right breast and his right hand gripped my left nipple as he bounced back and forth between the two like he was being breast-fed. I moaned louder and louder into his ear, turning him on more and more with every single sound. He stared into my eyes and moaned, "Rene, I love you."

Hearing those words made me tremble, and he once again proceeded to go back down South. I gyrated my hips and screamed louder and louder. "Fuck me, Vincent! Fuck me!" He waited until I couldn't take any more. I begged and begged for mercy. He knew exactly what it was that he was doing. I had no doubt about that. He pulled down his briefs and inserted his shaft. He pounded it until I had climaxed around the head of his dick several times.

The water had turned colder, and the showerhead, which I was still holding, was hurting my wrist from all the water pressure coming through. My legs were propped up in a funky position against the shower tile. My heart was racing, and I was trying to catch my breath in between. Damn. I couldn't believe that little thing could be used as such a tool. I placed it back on its piece and stepped out of the shower like nothing had happened at all.

I was enjoying spending time with myself lately. I knew what Rene wanted, what Rene needed. I knew that nobody could take my sexual appetite head-on like I could. I knew what turned me on and what turned me off. I knew how I liked to be licked and made love to. I wiped my body dry with a heavy white bath towel and then rubbed myself with body oil. The hazelnut scent and the vanilla extract made me smell as good as I felt. I blow-dried my hair and threw it in a ponytail that was slanting toward my left side. After that, I put on a thin nightie and waited for Vincent to return home. I looked at the grandfather clock. It was now 5:15 p.m. Dinner was ready to be eaten, and so was I.

Damn, Vincent. Where are you?

The telephone started ringing, and I damn near leaped over the couch in hopes of catching the call before it went to voice mail, praying it was my man. It was Shun.

"Hey, girl," I said.

"Damn. You sounding all happy. What's gotten into you?"

"Well, my new place, my new life, uh, and my new man."

She started laughing. "I see. Now, don't tell me I have to deal with this happy-go-lucky attitude when you come around me, making me feel all sad 'cause I ain't got a man. You know everybody ain't able."

I laughed. "I won't."

Rene

I could hear the garage door opening. Vincent had finally made it home. I hurried to turn off all the lights in the house. I had already made our plates and sat them on the dining table. I lit the two candles that I had standing parallel to each other. The dinner table was set. Vincent was coming in through the kitchen. I greeted him at the doorway.

"Hey, honey. You're back." I reached my arms around him, trying to steal me a kiss.

"Hey, babe."

"I hope you're hungry."

"Yeah. I can't wait to see what you've cooked up." He smiled.

I led him through the kitchen and into the dining room. I pulled out his chair, and he sat. I spread a cloth napkin over his lap, doing it the way he did when we went to a restaurant. He smiled up at me. I could see myself loving this man for the rest of my life. I took a seat. The candlelight bounced off his forehead as well as mine. There we sat, across from each other, gazing deeply into each other's eyes. I bowed my head to say grace.

"Amen."

We both picked up our forks, and his attention was still on me.

"So, what have you been doing since I've been gone?" I watched the way he used his knife to blindly separate the tender pieces of meat.

"Nothing. The usual woman stuff."

"The usual woman stuff? And what would that be?"

"I did a little shopping, cooked, cleaned, showered, and sat here in the dark, waiting for you to come home."

"Oh." He chewed a piece of meat and swallowed. "Delicious, Rene. Who taught you how to cook like this?"

I smiled, blushing a little. I had never told Vincent about me being raised in a foster home. All he knew was that I had been left with my grandmother and had been with her ever since.

"My grandma taught me," I lied. *There I go again. Dishing out lie after lie, like it is a natural thing for me.*

"Your grandmother taught you?" he repeated. "She surely knew what she was doing." I wished like hell that he would change the subject, if only for a minute. I hated having to lie to Vincent, but I had to in order to save my ass and my future. "You know what? It's been so selfish of me not to ask you this, but when do I get to meet that fine grandma of yours?"

I hurried and stuck a piece of roast in my mouth, then took my time to chew. I held up my index finger, as if to say, "Just one minute. Let me chew this first." He was still watching me, smiling and looking as good as could be. I tried to think of something real quick. I needed something to pop up in my brain. I thought about telling him she had passed away after he left, but I realized that would be so obviously stupid. The first thing he would think would be, *Your grandmother passed away, and you're sitting here, chowing down on some pot roast and potatoes*? I tossed that idea out the window. I couldn't think fast enough, so I did what I had seen some girl do on TV. I bit down on my tongue hard until my eyes watered. Then I grabbed my neck and started pointing to the kitchen.

"Water . . . water . . . ," I tried to say between gasps. I stood up, coughing and choking, trying to put on the best performance I could.

He rushed into the kitchen, opened the refrigerator, and rushed back with a bottle of Ozarka spring water. He tried to pat me on my back and help me cough up whatever it was that he thought was lodged in my throat. I spit out the piece of meat I had been chewing, and it landed on the floor, next to his foot.

"Thank you, honey!" I exclaimed.

"Are you all right?" He waited for me to catch my breath before I could talk again. I let out another cough for good measure. I grabbed the white napkin lying next to my plate and spit out the left-behind meat with a glob of saliva.

"I'm fine now, honey. Thank you."

He walked back over to his plate, removed it from the table, headed into the kitchen, and set the plate on the kitchen counter to be washed. I hoped that I hadn't spoiled his appetite, but from the looks of it, I had. I blew the candles out and switched on the lights.

"Let me go wash myself up," I said, embarrassed as hell.

I excused myself and went into the bathroom. *You're pathetic, Rene. Damn pathetic.* I brushed my teeth and gargled with the minty-tasting mouthwash that Vincent had on the counter. I looked in the mirror. It was ridiculous that I was going to such extremes not to be found out. A part of me wanted to just come clean about the grandma, Sand, and even about the baby. Acceptance and accountability were what I needed to embrace. It was hard trying to come up with a damn lie and excuse for every little thing. Lie after lie after lie. I almost couldn't keep up myself. I had told so many damn lies that I was turning blue in the damn face. And not telling Vincent about the baby was so beneath me. It was actually wrong as hell. He had never done anything to hurt me, and yet I was intentionally keeping things from him that would kill him if he found out. He would hate me for the rest of his life.

I stared at the confused woman in the mirror. I had to come clean. I hit the switch to turn off the lights and prepared myself for whatever it was that was due me. I deserved whatever my punishment would be. I felt ashamed, but I had to do what I knew was right. *Acceptance and accountability*, I repeated over and over.

There I stood, as ready as I could be to tell my fiancé, my future husband, that I was a phony. I was going to admit to him that everything he thought he knew about me was a complete lie. I bit down on my bottom lip and closed my eyes to brace myself for his reaction. I walked out of the bathroom and into the den. Vincent was flipping through channels, hoping to find something good on television to watch.

"Vincent, I need to talk to you." He looked up at me and then down again at the television. "Honey, I really need to talk to you." I walked over toward him, trying to grab his attention. I wanted no distractions, so I boldly stepped in front of the forty-two-inch-wide screen.

"Rene, what are you doing? I'm trying to watch this." He pointed the remote at the television, boosted the volume so he could still hear what he could partially see. I remained in my position, refusing to move.

"Vincent," I said in such a low, guilty tone. "I have something I need to tell you." I decided to start with the baby. "Vincent, I . . . I . . . lost the bbbbaa . . ." I struggled to say what it was that I had to say. The words were somehow caught in my throat.

"Rene!" he yelled.

I jumped.

"Babe, I can't see through you." He was trying to watch some damn baseball game, and I was trying to tell him that I had lost our child.

"I need to talk to you, Vincent." I was damn near pleading with him. The look on my face was evident. I needed to say this while I still had the strength and the courage to do so. He swayed his head in different directions, trying to watch television through me, as if he had some sort of X-ray vision. He wasn't successful. "Fuck it," I said, hoping he didn't hear me.

I headed for the bedroom, plopped down on the king-size mattress, and allowed my mind to wander off. I thought about how my life was so miserably perplexing. I didn't know if I was gay, bisexual, or straight. All I knew was that I was looking for change but wasn't sure if I could just forget about my past that quickly and with such ease. As hard as I had tried to put Sand in the back of my mind, she still existed, and erasing her from my memory was not possible. I had fooled myself into thinking that her having someone else in her life would make me hate her and never, ever want to see her again. It had done just the opposite. Instead of wishing she got ran over by an 18-wheeler or, better yet, struck by lightning, I was hoping she would forgive me and take me back.

My conscience was beginning to whup my ass, and I faced the fact that Sand owned my heart. The score was even. I had cheated on her, and she had cheated on me. One back washed the other. I grabbed the phone that was lying next to Vincent's side of the bed and punched in her digits. First, I tried the home phone. I was greeted by my own voice.

Damn. I hadn't realized that I am so damn long-winded. That is a long-ass greeting, I told myself.

I quickly hung up before the beeping sound came on. I had intentionally blocked my number by pressing *67, so there was no way she could trace the call back here. I hurriedly dialed her cell and waited for her to pick up. When she didn't, I became worried. Sand hardly ever let her phone ring without answering it to see who was calling. It could have been a connect or maybe me. It continuously rang and rang. I disconnected the call. Where was she? Then, suddenly, a picture of her girlfriend flashed in my mind. I slammed the phone down and knew that she was somewhere laid up under that ho.

I tried to control my emotions; after all, I had brought this on myself. I needed to see her. I wanted to see her. I had to tell her that I was sorry for all the shit I had kept hidden from her. I wanted to tell her that the letter I had left for her was written out of anger and to pretend she had never read it. I was still in love with Sand, and I couldn't play myself any longer. The shit was real. Our love was real.

It was about seven o'clock, judging by the way the room had darkened since I'd come in. I still had time to find her and tell her that I loved her. I could beg for forgiveness, and she would take me back with open arms. I would tell her about Vincent, the baby, and how all these years I had denied that I was gay but had known deep down that I was. I quickly threw some clothes in a blue and red duffel bag. I slipped on some jeans and an old Nike shirt, one that I generally wore around the house to lounge in. I slipped on my tennis shoes and grabbed my purse. I almost made it past Vincent without him seeing me. My shadow across the television screen busted me out.

"Where you going?"

I stopped dead in my tracks and turned to face the back of his head. He was still watching me in the TV.

"I, um, um, gotta go sit with Shun. She's at the hospital. Jo Jo sick with the flu," I lied. I didn't know what I was so

nervous about, but my underarms were starting to per-
spire and my pubic hairs already had my thong clinging
to them, I was sweating so hard. You would think I was
used to lying, the way it had become so ordinary, like an
English professor's fluency with English.

"Well, it's dark out, so you need to be careful."

"Okay. I will. I won't be gone long." I tried to haul ass
out that front door, but he stopped me again.

"Rene." He sprang up from the couch and walked
toward me. I didn't know what he was about to do. I was
scared as hell, and I didn't even know why. He lifted up
my shirt and bent down to kiss my stomach. I sighed
softly. "What are we now? Almost three months?"

I just nodded my head yes. I couldn't take this anymore. "Baby, I gotta go. Shun needs me." I walked out
the front door and left him standing alone. I called Shun
from a prepaid phone I had bought earlier at the grocery
store. I had to warn her not to call the house.

"Why I always gotta be your scapegoat?" she spat.

"Because that's what friends do."

"Where are you going, anyways?"

I paused before I could say anything. I knew how
much Shun hated to see Sand and me together. I knew
she disapproved of our relationship. She was rooting for
my life of fake happiness with Vincent, even though she
knew my heart was with Sand. She had tried to convince
me that Vincent would just make me forget all about
Sand with the swerve of his dick. I had tested the waters.
I had even envisioned Sand's head in between my legs,
replacing Vincent's dick, but the shit still hadn't worked.
Yes, he had a dick, but that was all that he had to classify
him as a real man, which was what I had figured I needed
society to see. I wasn't sure if it was just that I hadn't been
able to get what I wanted from him because I compared
him so much to Sand or if it wasn't working all around
and I was still trying to find a reason to stay.

I had exhausted myself so much from telling lies that I decided to just come out and be honest with Shun.

"I'm gonna find Sand." There was a brief silence.

"Rene, you are making a big mistake. Vincent loves you. What are you doing?"

"Shun, with all due respect, I don't need you to tell me who I need to be with. I listen to you constantly go on and on about Sand and me. The truth is, I'm tired of it. You bash on her in my face, but she's no different than I am. I love her, and I know she loves me. Understand that I don't need you or anybody else telling me who or what I need to be with. This is my life, not yours. I'll sleep with whoever I wanna. If nobody likes it, they can kiss my caramel ass!"

She was quiet, but I could still hear her heavy breathing. Then she said, "I just don't want you to throw away a good thing. A man like Vincent is hard to find. She cheated on you, for God's sake. Have some dignity."

That was the last draw. I had had it. She would never understand it, and it wasn't my place to make her. I disconnected the call. Immediately after that, Vincent was calling me on the new number I had left on the coffee table without him seeing.

"Hello?"

"Rene, I forgot to tell you, when you get back home tonight, I have a surprise for you."

"What? A Surprise?"

"I was meaning to give it to you earlier, but I had to make sure that my partner would come through on his end of the bargain. And he did. He just called."

"Honey, you're spoiling me," I replied in a sweet, innocent voice.

"No, I'm not spoiling you enough. I love you, Rene."

I held the phone to my ear, letting the tears drip down my face. I needed to tell him before it was too late. "Vincent, I love you too. I just don't think I deserve—"

"Stop. I don't want to hear that. You deserve everything I have planned for you. Believe me, it's all worth it."

"Honey," I said between sniffles, "I'll talk to you later."

"All right. See you later. Call me when you reach your destination."

"I will."

I pulled up into my old parking space. I had been away only for a day, but it seemed like an eternity. I ran up the flight of stairs, with the duffel bag in tow. I unlocked the door and barged in, wanting to catch some tramp ho up in my shit so I could act a fool on her ass. Everything was exactly how I had left it, except there was a crystal glass missing from the bar rack. I spotted it immediately. I rushed to the kitchen sink, and there it was. I inspected it for lipstick. There wasn't any. Sand and I used the crystal glasses only for company. And I was not talking friends. I was talking "run and clean everything till it's spotless" company.

I walked around the small apartment, giving it a once-over. You would have thought I was just moving in the way I was checking everything out. I walked over to the caller ID and checked for any new calls. There were several. I didn't recognize any of the numbers, so I skipped over them, scrolling to the next. None for me. I picked up the phone and decided to call Sand. Once again she did not answer. This time, I felt the need to leave a message.

"Hey, hon," I teased, throwing on the sexiest phone voice I could put on. She was bound to run home after hearing that. I whispered something nice and sweet. I headed to the bathroom to shower again after all that sweating I had done earlier. Then I threw on one of her muscle T-shirts and walked around the house in a shirt and panties, anticipating the makeup sex. I was getting moist just thinking about it.

Sand

The moment I pulled into the parking lot, I spotted all the commotion. There was a long-ass line that had begun to curve around the building. Everybody was waiting impatiently to get inside and see for themselves what all the hype was about.

I parked my car in the reserved section, which had been intentionally blocked off with orange cones. As soon as my boy Reginald saw me, he ran over.

"Damn, Sand, we got a house full, and people still tryin'a get in." He was as excited as I was about the grand opening.

"That's good. That's real good," I repeated. I was pleased to know that. He was the fifth person I had keeping count of every single head that entered my building. One of the reasons was that I didn't want to create a fire hazard, and another was that I would know exactly how much money I should be counting at the end of the night. "Well, when we reach our max, close the doors and don't let nobody else in."

"All right. I gotcha." He ran back to his post.

I slipped my way on through the crowd and inside the doors, where all my hard work was invested. DJ Sparks had the place rockin'. The vibration of the speakers had everybody up on their feet. You couldn't help but join in on the dance floor and shake your ass. The first performing artist, Lil Jon & the East Side Boyz, hyped up the crowd with their rap lyrics. Fans who had rehearsed the song were able to sing along, as well as throw in their own dance routine. I took a glance around the place. Black bulbs were in all the light fixtures, except for those surrounding the six bars and above the dance floor. Those were multicolored strobe lights shining down. Anyone who wore all white or neon colors would surely be the center of attention for the night, including me. I was dressed down in solid white and had removed the black and green beads from the ends of my hair and replaced them with white ones. I was g'd up, most definitely.

I continued to check out the club, making sure all the bouncers and undercover security officers were in place and on duty. They were. I checked over each bar, ensuring that the attendants were handling that end and that the waitresses were on their jobs. The bartenders knew the drill: no watered-down shit, but don't make 'em pass out. I knew from doing my research that the bar cash was where the money was at. So for that reason, we had everything in the book, from Cristal, Moët, and Hpnotiq to basic gin and juice. I estimated that I'd rake in at least forty grand just in liquor tonight.

Everyone appeared to be having a good time. Sandrene's was on blaze. Finally, I headed to the spot where I knew I'd camp out for most of the night—the VIP. I made my way through the crunk crowd and headed to the ballas' section of the club. The VIP room was sectioned off from the rest of the club, but those who were inside were still able to see what was going on outside the room. A two-sided mirror allowed you to see the other side, while those outside of the VIP would mistake the long glass for a regular mirror and would see their reflection. That was the cool part of the VIP. And while the outside had hidden security cameras, the VIP did not.

The room was decorated nicely in a black-and-white zebra print that matched the marble tile on the outside dance floor. Inside of the VIP was a bar, a pool table, a big-screen television, and leather sectional sofas and chairs throughout. I had let the decorator do her own thing, and I had to admit, it was hot. I really liked it. Everything matched perfectly. I made my way around the room, introducing myself to everyone, including the high rollers who had come through to check out the new spot.

The VIP also had its own DJ. He was an older cat, but he knew music like no one else. He would mix it up a little, taking it from new age to old school every other track. I checked my watch. It was ten minutes past eleven. The party was just beginning. I walked past a few of the ladies who must have been invited into the VIP. Certain ladies had been hand selected to roam around the VIP all night if they wanted. They didn't have to pay. They had a purpose, and I had mine. The more they could get the fellas to spend that money and buy them drinks all night long, the more revenue I was kicking in. I made sure that the finest ladies in the building were escorted inside the VIP for free. Three of the finest were standing right in front of me, staring out through the glass, watching the peep show from indoors. They looked too damn good not to be seen and flaunted around this muthafucka, so I had to volunteer my services.

"You ladies doing all right tonight?" I had a sweet smile spread across my face.

"Yes, we fine," one of them answered.

"Can I offer y'all a drink or something?"

"Not right now. We don't wanna get too tipsy. We already had one," the same one said. She showed me her glass.

"All right. If you sexy ladies need anything, you just holler at me, a'ight?"

All three of them blushed. "All right," they chorused.

I could tell who the leader of the pack was, because she was the only one speaking and was speaking for all. That told me a lot about her. She was aggressive, knew exactly what she wanted, and liked to be in control. The type of woman I had promised myself never to get involved with again, especially after fucking with Jasmine.

I walked off, picked up the pace, but I was tempted to look back at her one more time. She looked so damn good in that sleek orange dress, with her weave flowing down her back. Yes, she was watching me, and again, I was turned on. "I'm irresistible," I said aloud, flattering myself with my own cocky attitude and ego. I stepped over to the bar and requested my usual—a glass of vodka, my liquid painkiller and stress release.

As I allowed the liquid to coat my throat warmly, my thoughts shifted to other things. I tried to shake off the chilling voice of the person who had called me earlier, but I couldn't. I tried to erase the words that Shun had said to me. Rene was involved with someone else, and that someone else was a man. I couldn't believe that. I just couldn't. The idea of it made me go crazy. I brought the glass back to my lips and took another swallow, this time finishing the glass.

"Hit me again," I told the bartender. The vision was too much to handle. Rene and another man was impossible. She would never do anything like that. Shun was a liar, anyway. I took another hard hit, tossing the drink up like it was cherry-flavored Kool-Aid. Then I remembered what Peaches had told me, and I was forced to down the rest of my drink. I shook my head at the fact that James and Chyna were trying to set me up for some shit I didn't do. But I couldn't figure out why.

I was back to feeling alone. I walked around a little bit more to feel out the crowd in the VIP. I spotted Nessa with no problem. She had on an animal-print jacket and a nice little pantsuit with a matching cowgirl hat. She had it going on. I made my way over to where she was sitting. She was glowing under the fluorescent lights.

"Sup, baby girl?" I said as I sat down next to her.

"Nothing." She appeared a little amazed by everything that was going on.

"Where your girl at?"

Nessa looked back up at me with a smile on her face. "She here."

I looked around, hoping to see her.

"She went to the restroom. She'll be back."

"Oh."

She looked at me like I was up to something.

"What?" I asked, smiling at her.

"Don't even play. I know what that little smirk across you face mean, Sand. You ain't fooling nobody."

"What smirk?" I said, denying the obvious. I laughed and continued to play dumb.

"Um, yeah, the smirk that says you like my friend." Nessa giggled a little. "But don't worry. The feelings are mutual."

"What? You know something I don't?" I asked as I tapped her on the leg.

"My secret is quiet as kept." She started laughing, then placed her right index finger to her lips.

"Come on. Don't do me like that," I begged.

She shook her head. "Nope, nope, nope."

"All right. I got you when it comes tip time."

That got her attention. She looked up. "Okay, wait, wait, wait. Promise me you won't say anything."

"Come on, Nessa. You can trust me."

"All right. Deja likes you. She really likes you."

I started smiling. "Shit, I thought you had something to tell me. She bound to like me. I'm a likable person."

She elbowed me in the side, and I pretended to be hurt.

"I'm moving over here. You dangerous." I slid onto the love seat across from her. She started laughing, but I had seen Deja turn the corner, and I was hoping she would sit next to me on the love seat.

"Hey, Sand. You doing all right tonight?" Deja said as she approached us.

I stood up, making space for her to slide in next to me or take a seat with Nessa. She sat on the love seat, where she had seen me sitting. I sat back down next to her.

"I'm fine, Ms. Lady," I replied, calling her after my car, respecting her and caring for her like I did my ride. "How are you tonight?"

She looked over at Nessa, who had her attention focused elsewhere. "I'm all good now." She looked back at me. After what Nessa had told me, I could read in between the lines of that statement. I decided to throw her a curveball.

"That's good, Ma. I hope you stay all good, because you know you look it."

She smiled and blushed so much she couldn't look me in the face.

"Are you ladies thirsty?" I asked, quickly after sensing a little discomfort from her. I knew that some gay women really didn't like to share or flaunt their business in public and make a scene, so I eased back a little and revised my approach.

"Yes, I would like a glass of chardonnay, if you have it," Deja replied.

"And what would you like, Nes?" I asked, slicing her name in half to sound more like a longtime friend.

"Whatever is gon' give me the balls to walk over to that sexy chocolate muthafucka over there." She pointed hesitantly at the other side of the room. I followed her finger. There stood James, posted up in a corner, in an all-black suit. He bounced his head up at me when we made eye contact. I looked away and back down at Nessa, who was damn near squirming in her seat. She must have gotten herself wet the way she kept shifting her legs from one side to the other. "Ooh and that bald head. Goddamn. I need my drink, Sand."

I walked over to the bar, grabbed two filled glasses, and brought them back over to them.

"I'll be right back," I told them.

"Okay," they both said in unison.

What the fuck is he doing here? Everything that Peaches had told me was still fresh in my mind. I hoped this punk muthafucka wasn't bold enough to step to me in my place of business over no ho shit. I knew he wouldn't, because he wouldn't dare get that Stacy Adams suit of his dirtied up. I remained calm and walked over to him.

"This a nice place you got here, Sand," he said, looking over the club. "What happened to you Wednesday night? You missed the domino game me and the guys had going. They were asking me where my partner was. I ended up partnering with Malik, and you know that nigga can't play no bones. Shit, I lost two dubs."

"Man, I been tied up with other shit."

"Um, I heard that." He was looking over my shoulder at Nessa, who, I imagined, was still being flirty. "Who that shorty over there in the catsuit?" he asked, referring to Nessa.

"That's my homegirl. She braids my hair."

"Damn, she fine. She better be lucky I'm engaged."

I wanted to make sure I had heard him right. "Engaged?" I repeated.

"Yeah, your boy decided he gon' settle on down and tie the knot."

Man, this shit was blowing my mind. I chilled out, trying to maintain my cool. I couldn't let him know that I had already been hipped to his and Chyna's little scheme. He wasn't as slick as he thought he was.

"Engaged, huh?" I said for the second time.

"Yep. I almost can't believe it my damn self."

I smiled as I pondered my next move. "And what you say her name was again?" I knew this would get him.

"Hey, hey, hey, can I get another one of these?" He was waving down the waitress who had just passed us by.

"You sure can, Daddy."

"Damn, they know how to treat a brother up in here, and you ain't gotta be no damn million-dollar-having nigga, either." He was smiling. "My nig, I'm gonna go on over here and get on this pool game before these chicks get me in some trouble." He totally avoided my question all the way around. I knew it. I just knew it. Peaches was telling the truth. I smiled a fake-ass smile.

"A'ight, dog. I'm a holla at you later, then." I walked away. "Fake-ass nigga," I mumbled loud enough for the waitress returning with his drink to hear. She looked at me and then went on back to work. I headed back to my guests.

Deja was enticing. She had on a shimmering gold dress with a matching earring and necklace set. She looked extra sexy tonight, and I was sure she knew it.

"Are you enjoying yourself?" I asked. I didn't want to damn myself by holding eye contact with her for longer than a minute, because then I'd be under the hypnotic spell of her beauty. And that had to be dangerous. I couldn't help it, though. I stared into her eyes. Goddamn it. I wanted her.

"Yes, I am. Thanks for asking."

"My pleasure."

She smiled, and that just made my night.

The night was going real well. I was able to get in a few dances with Nessa and Deja. Deja really knew how to move, but I could tell she was more comfortable with the slow jams. I wanted to see her bounce that ass, like the rapper yelling from the speakers was telling her to do, but I was also pleased with the way she slow wound in front of me, moving her body like a snake and then dropping it like it was hot. She was getting loose, and so was Nessa, except Nessa was across the dance floor, giving it what she had for a pork chop. That damn girl came back sweating, she had danced so hard. Man, the place was so damn crunk. I made a mental note to tell Julia, the chick I had helping me out with all the payroll checks, to give the DJ something extra. He was cutting up.

Hours later I woke up to Deja to the left of me, in the driver's seat. She was chauffeuring me home, but what the hell for? She looked down at me when she saw me raise the seat up from its comfortable reclined position.

"Too many drinks, huh?" Deja asked.

I wiped my blurry eyes with the sleeve of my shirt. "What's going on?" I asked. I sat up straighter, relinquishing my slouched position. It took me a second to realize she was pushing my whip. I guessed the look on my face told her what I was thinking.

"Don't worry. I ain't gonna bang your rims on the curb." She smiled.

Was I that damn drunk? I asked myself, because I couldn't remember shit. I grabbed at my head, which was pounding so hard. Everything was starting to look blurry again. I felt myself dozing off, going right back to sleep.

Beep! Beep! Beep!

I jumped up, knocking the blanket on the floor. It was cold as hell. I immediately broke out in chills. I looked around, trying to make out where I was. Nothing looked familiar. I stood. I smelled smoke. Something was on fire. The smoke detectors had detected that. They were still going off. I opened what appeared to be a bedroom door, and a cloud of smoke greeted me. *Where was I?* I followed the smell. It led me into a smoke-filled kitchen. There was Deja, in some pink and white pajamas and white crew socks, with her hair in a black silk scarf. She was removing the oven mitts that she had on. I looked on the stove top. There was a once silver pan, which was now charcoal black, and I assumed that was bacon that was burned inside of it.

What the hell is she trying to do? Burn us both up? How do you burn baked bacon?

"Hey, sleepyhead," she said when she spotted me.

Even in the morning she was beautiful. She walked over to me and grabbed my hands, then pulled me into the kitchen. She pulled out a bar stool that was sitting in front of the island. She took out a placemat, two plates, and forks. I watched her fill both plates with scrambled eggs and cheese, oatmeal, charred bacon, and some fluffy buttermilk biscuits. "I know the bacon's a little crispy, but it's all good." She smiled. She poured me a glass of orange juice and a glass of skim milk for herself.

"Deja, what am I doing at your place?" I knew she wanted me, but damn, I didn't know she was willing to kidnap my ass. She looked at me like she was shocked at my question.

"You really don't remember?"

"No."

She stared at me in disbelief. "Sand, you passed out."

"What!"

"You passed out."

That was impossible. I'd gotten drunk on many occasions, and I ain't never passed the hell out.

"Me and Nessa were trying to wake you, but you were unresponsive. You wouldn't say anything."

I couldn't believe that shit. That was embarrassing. I had never done no shit like that.

"Did you take anything before you went to the club?"

"No," I said. I thought back to everything I had done before I went to the club.

"Well, I don't know what in the hell happened. My guess was that you just had way too much to drink." She bit into a piece of that blackened bacon.

"So why'd you bring me here?" I asked her. I looked around her place and then back at her. I bit into the biscuit.

"Where else were you gonna go? I'm not that cruel. I wanted to make sure you were okay, and since I had ridden with Nessa to the club, I just thought I should drive your car here so you wouldn't wake up frantic about your ride. She pointed out her living room window, and I could see my car parked safely in her driveway, next to her red Honda Civic.

"Thanks for looking out," I said. I stared into her eyes once again, trying to figure out why she even cared at all. Anybody else would have left me there. Rene had done that. My parents had done that. "So, you live alone?" I asked her. The place was so neat and clean that I was sure that she was the only person staying here.

"Yeah, I'm all by my lonesome."

"So your girlfriend's not staying here to keep you company?"

She looked up at me in a peculiar way, with her milk mustache and all. "My, aren't we nosy?" She licked the film of milk off her upper lip.

"I just don't want to intrude or anything. I mean, she might pop up and be like, 'Who this nigga up in my girl shit?' That's all I'm saying."

"Well, you don't have to worry about that. I'm not seeing anyone right now." She paused. "My ex kinda left me to be with someone else." She looked away from me. I figured it was probably something she preferred not to discuss. I tried to change the topic of conversation.

"Fuck, I can't believe I got that damn drunk. I was fucked up, huh?"

She started laughing. "Yeah, you were past tipsy."

"Damn. So I guess my girl don't be joking when she calls me an alcoholic." My eyes once again roamed around her kitchen. I needed a Black. I pulled a single cigar from the box that was still in my back pocket. "Hey, I'ma go step outside and smoke this," I told her.

"You ain't gotta go nowhere." She stood to her feet, walked up beside me, and lit the cigar with her cigarette lighter. "You smoke weed?"

I pretended to be looking around for someone else. "You asking me?"

She nodded her head.

"Shit. Hell, yeah. Where the killa at?"

She pulled out a fat-ass sack that she had stashed in her kitchen drawer. It was early in the morning, but we were about to blaze. I would have never been able to do some shit like this with Rene. She would kill me if I even smoked a cigarette in the house, let alone some killa. Deja rolled the joint like a professional who had been doing it for some time. I took a strong puff, inhaling the smoke. The product tasted familiar, almost like the shit I had sold and smoked with James on occasion. I pursed my lips and let the indo slip from my mouth and into thin air. It was all good. After a few more puffs of the herb, I could feel my eyes starting to get tight and the high beginning to settle in. Deja was hitting the blunt like a muthafucka, cheefing like it was something she practiced on a regular basis.

"What?" she asked after catching me staring at her. "Never seen somebody get high before?"

She looked even hotter to me. She offered me a glass of fruit punch that she had quickly whipped together. That shit was good. I licked the moisture from my top lip.

"Did you like that?"

"Yeah, sure did. Is there more where that came from?"

"It depends on how thirsty you are."

"Is that right? Well in that case, I feel a little dehydrated." She smiled. Oh, how I could go on, but I was only teasing myself. Wasn't no way I was about to get down with this girl, but I saw no harm in a little fun.

I was still thinking about Rene. I wondered where she was at this very moment. I missed her so much. I desperately needed to hear that she was okay. Just then, a vibration from her cell shot through my pocket. I pulled out her phone, which I was still carrying around on me for calling purposes, since I had tossed mine out on the freeway, into moving traffic. I answered it.

"Hello."

"Hello. Who is this?" The raspy, congested-sounding voice couldn't have belonged to anyone other than Shun.

"What you want, Shun?" I asked, irritated at the sound of her voice. I tilted the phone away from my ear because she talked loud as hell and she wasn't about to bust my damn eardrums out. At the mention of a female's name, Deja stood up and walked away, feeling the need to leave me in privacy.

"Why the hell are you answering Rene's phone?"

"Man, don't worry about all that," I said. "I pay this damn phone bill. I can answer it whenever I get ready."

She hissed, "You know what? You're ruining it for Rene. I care about her happiness too much to continue to watch you stand in the way of the perfect life that she is destined to have, if she could just rid herself of your ass.

You don't know how to make her happy. Shit, you can't even give her the family she wants." The remarks Shun made were aimed at my heart, like an arrow piercing through human flesh. "Rene deserves to be happy." It sounded like she was on the verge of breaking down in tears. "I want what's best for her!" she screamed.

What had given her the idea that I was not concerned about what was best for Rene? Hell, I had made sure Rene had what she wanted and everything that she needed. Where the fuck was she when Rene was looking for a shoulder to cry on? Where the fuck was she on the third of the month, when rent was due? Where in the fuck was she when the transmission needed to be rebuilt? I was the one footing everything.

"Shun, I don't know what the hell you talking about," I blurted, sadness building in my voice.

"Tell her you moved on, so her and Vincent can have another baby." That made me raise up from my seat.

"What!" I yelled into the phone, making Deja flinch a bit.

"You heard me. You're nothing but the damn devil. Let that girl move on with her life, and quit trying to get in the way." *Click.* She had hung the phone up in my face. I was mad as hell, but the tears that were rolling down my cheeks said otherwise.

Deja ran over to me. "What's wrong, Sand? Are you okay? What happened?"

I jerked away, refusing to let her see me like this. I grabbed my car keys from the end table and walked out the door. I got in my car and backed out of her driveway. I looked in my rearview mirror at the blurry vision of Deja left behind, standing on the front of her doorstep, still wearing her pajamas, clueless as to what was going on. Tears raced down my face even quicker. I was already down the street and two exits away from the apartment.

I stopped at the red light, signaling to make a left turn. *Come on, light.* Within half a second, I looked up in the rearview, and an old white van appeared out of nowhere, coming right at me at full speed.

Rene

Hearing the door shut was what woke me up from my sleep. A wide smile crossed my face because I knew Sand had finally made it home. I glanced over at the clock like usual when I was about to drill her on her whereabouts. It was a quarter till one. Tonight was going to be different. No arguments, no bad-mouthing each other, just the sweet sounds and essence of love-making and passionate sex filling the room. I imagined her squeezing my ass so tight and kissing me like she never had before. Tonight I would submit and let her enjoy having her way with me. I would take back all the horrible shit I had said about her, to her, and had thought about her.

It was interesting how someone could just turn you against somebody because they were jealous of your happiness, afraid that they would never find that special someone who loved them as much as they deserved and needed to be loved. Sand was that special someone for me. I had been crazy to think differently. I lay quietly, naked under clean linen sheets, ready to surprise her in my birthday suit. Once she pulled back the covers, my nakedness would be exposed and she would react to how my round, pointy, mahogany brown, juicy tenders screamed out her name. I was getting excited just fantasizing about the premeditated moment. Yes, the moistness that I felt between my legs confirmed my realities—all my realities.

I heard keys rattling and heavy footsteps. I wanted to give her a warning about the mood I was in. If she didn't feel the steam coming from underneath the door, then once she entered the bedroom, she was destined to get scorched. I was hot as hell. I reached for the remote, cranked the volume up on the radio some more. She should get the idea now. I lay back, pretending not to know she was home. I pulled the covers up to my chin and closed my eyes. I felt her body getting closer and closer. I lay still on my back, knowing the thin sheets showed the impression of my fully aroused breasts.

Don't peek, I kept telling myself. I used my senses to create an image in my mind of what she had on and how sexy she looked standing over me right now. I couldn't take it anymore. I opened my eyes. A tall, large body dressed in all black, with a black ski mask covering the face, stood in front of me. I quickly rose up, backed away from the masked intruder. I was terrified.

He lifted one of his index fingers to his lips and slowly shook his head sideways. He was warning me not to scream. Although it did cross my mind, I knew it would only get me killed. I was frantic. I began shaking all over from just from his frightening presence. I looked down at his glove-covered hands and immediately realized this man was here to hurt me. This was real. I was scared to death. My heart began pounding faster as I tried with all my might to remain calm and not make a peep. A stranger was in my home, and he was dressed to kill. I pulled the covers closer to me, attempting to hide my naked body. The masked man snatched the sheet from my hands and threw it onto the floor.

I quickly balled myself up in the fetal position, knees damn near pushed into my chest, pressing up against my tits, to keep from exposing myself to him. I was so afraid of what he planned to do to me. The only thought running through my mind was that I was going to die. Lord knows I didn't want to die like this. I wanted to die from natural causes, not murder. I wanted to holler for help, but it would be impossible for anyone to hear me over the loud music. I wasn't sure what to do. I began worrying more. Finally, I opted to bargain with the masked man and try to negotiate for my young life. I wanted to piss myself the longer I stared into a face that had not been revealed to me.

Before I could open my mouth and offer him every dime I had, he gave me instructions on what not to do. Don't say anything."

I became even more nervous. My eyes followed him closely as I tried to predict what was going to happen to me. He looked around my room. Finally, he bent down, picked up the sheet, and tore it straight down the middle. Then he dropped one half of the sheet on the floor and split the other half in two.

"Hold out your arms," he demanded. He tied one part of the ripped sheet tightly around my arms.

"Please . . . please," I begged. "I have ten thousand dollars in the bank. You can have it all. Just please don't hurt me."

He was silent, which scared me even more. He took the other half of the second part of the sheet he had ripped and tied it around my mouth. Mumbles were all he could hear coming out of my mouth. My watery eyes begged him to let me go. They also said, "I am gonna cooperate and not try any dumb shit, so please just free me."

He took a cell phone out of his pocket and placed a call. My heart began to race even faster than before. *Sand, where are you?* was all I kept thinking.

"I got her." The intruder was watching me through the slits in his mask. "Yes, we're alone. Okay. I can do that."

He flipped the phone closed and stuck it back in his pocket. "Somebody wanted me to deliver a little message to you." He gripped me by the hair and brought my face up to his. The small amount of air he blew through his mask was enough to make my nose turn up on its own. "You want some real dick? You wanna get fucked real hard?" He pushed my head to the side and began unzipping his pants.

I kicked and kicked until all my strength was gone. "Please," I kept trying to yell. No matter how loud I screamed, there was no one who would hear me. My screams were muffled whimpers.

"Shut the fuck up, bitch!" He slapped me. I fell back. He climbed on top of me, his mask still on his face. I lay back and prayed to God that he was not about to do what I thought he was. "Spread them legs and let me show you what a real dick feels like."

He forced my legs apart.

I struggled to close them.

He slapped me again.

"Open up, bitch! Don't act like you scared of the dick now." He was finally able to get in between my legs. I was still crying, scared for my dear life. He removed his gloves. He ran his nasty fingers across me freely. First over my breasts and then down my stomach. When he came to my middle area, he stopped. "You know, you're a waste of a woman. I see why my man paid me to fuck you up. All this good dick walking around, and you'd rather have a bitch who wished she had a dick. Any other bitch would kill to have a big dick like this swinging up in 'em every night, deep strokin' that pussy."

When he said the word *kill*, I knew I was about to die. That was the only thing I heard come out of his mouth. He suddenly shoved his bare dick roughly inside my dry, tight hole without warning. It hurt so bad. I cried, but no one could hear me with the sheet tied around my mouth. I couldn't even hear myself. *Dear Jesus, dear Lord*, I prayed.

He pumped and pounded his dick in and out, intentionally roughing me up, and then finally grabbed me by the neck when he was ready to release. His grip was so strong that I thought he was trying to choke me into an orgasm of my own. I tried to catch as many breaths as I could, because he was strangling me. All of a sudden, I felt a warm gush let go inside of me and his hard, huge body convulsed. I couldn't stomach the stinky smell coming from his musty balls and his funky breath, which he continuously blew in my face once he reached his stolen peak. He struggled to his feet, grabbed one end of the sheet, and began wiping his nasty sweat, which had dripped from under his mask onto my uncovered chest. I scooted away from him as far as I could, moving toward the other side of the bed, when he got up. He saw that I was in pain, but he didn't care. I couldn't keep from crying. I felt so violated.

He shook off the slime that was dripping from his dick, forced it back into his pants, and slid the gloves back on. "So, how you want it, baby girl? Slow and painful or quick and painless?"

I shook my head, indicating neither. I didn't want to die. Even though, for a split second I wished I was dead, because I was in so much agonizing pain.

As he waited for me to decide my fate, there was a loud-ass knock on the door, which startled both of us.

"Who the fuck is that?" he demanded.

I shrugged my shoulders. I had no idea who it was or who it could be.

Up until that point, he hadn't presented a weapon, but hearing that knock made him pull one out. I had never seen a gun up close before. It was black all over, and it fit tightly between his trigger-happy fingers. He pointed it in my face. "Get rid of 'em." He pulled me up on my feet. "Any funny shit and I'll blow your fuckin' head off, bitch," he reminded me.

The knocks got stronger and louder. He searched the room, trying to find something for me to slip on. He hurried and untied the sheet over my mouth and then the one tied around my arms. He tossed me one of my long nightgowns that he found in the laundry basket near the closet. I slipped it over my head, still hurting and in pain. In between my legs felt like it was on fire, and so did my wrists, where they had been tied tightly for so long.

I walked to the front door. He followed me, standing right behind me but keeping himself out of view.

"Who is it?" I asked in a shaky voice. The gun was pointed right at my side. I knew that if I made any crazy gestures or movements, he would shoot me in the gut and would probably finish me off with a head shot.

"It's Dallas police, ma'am. Could you open your door please?"

I looked to the right side of me, where the robber or killer—I wasn't sure what to call him—was calmly standing. He pulled his finger up to his lips and then waved the gun as a reminder of what was to come next if I said anything. I opened the door slowly. Two uniformed Dallas police officers stood there, holding flashlights, and one had his hand positioned on his weapon, in case he needed to pull it out real quick. The tall officer shined the light in my face, looked over my shoulder to see if he could see anything. He lowered it when he saw the light was nearly blinding me.

"Ma'am, we received two complaints about loud music coming from this unit."

"I, uh, didn't realize I had it up so loud. I will turn it off, Officer. I sorta fell asleep with it on like that," I lied. I couldn't hide the fear in my eyes. *Please don't leave me,* I thought. *This guy is gonna kill me.*

The black officer spoke up. "Ma'am, can I get your name?"

"It's . . . uh . . . uh . . . Rene Montgomery. I mean, it's Rene Brown."

He gave the white officer a strange look.

The white officer spoke again. "Miss Brown, do you live at this residence?"

"Yes, sir. I just moved back in yesterday." I pulled my hair behind my ears, nervous as hell. I wished I could volunteer that I had two tickets that I hadn't paid, if that was going to get me arrested and away from this crazy muthafucka right next to me. But I still felt the gun pointing in my direction, so I kept my mouth shut.

"Officer Brinkley, we have a disturbance call. . . ." The white officer lowered the volume on his radio, nearly ignoring the dispatcher call.

"Are you okay, miss? You look a little distressed," the black officer said.

"I'm fine," I lied.

"All right, just keep it down. Folks are trying to get some sleep."

"I will," I told him.

He looked me in my eyes and then winked. I didn't know what that could possibly mean. They both walked off quickly, hurrying down the steps. When I couldn't see their uniforms anymore, I began to panic all over again. I was about to die. I slowly closed the door and was face-to-face with this monster.

"That's my girl," he said, applauding me with the gun in his hand. "You know what? I like the way you obey. Let's go back in this room and pick up where we left off. I think I want my dick sucked real good." He nodded his head up and down excitedly. I felt so fucking sick to my stomach.

"Go on. Get back there." He pushed me in the back of my head.

I looked to the left of me, where he was, and suddenly saw the reason the officer had winked at me. He had seen my situation. He had seen that I had a gun pointed at me, ready to blow my damn brains out. My large gold-framed mirror that hung in the dining area had shown him everything. He had seen the intruder. I was going to be okay. I just had to play along and not do anything stupid.

I was already gagging before the tip of his penis even touched my lips. I was crying and begging him not to make me do it. He pointed the gun at me, using it to intensify the threat of him blowing my head off.

"Think you too good to suck a nigga dick, huh? Bitch, mouth my shit."

I was on my knees, quivering with fear, being ordered to perform oral sex on this fuckin' bastard who had just broken into my house. Dying wasn't an option for me, so I had to oblige. I placed my untrained lips around the head of his penis, felt it swell inside my mouth once it entered.

"Yeah, open that mouth on up." He was enjoying himself, while I hated every single second of it. He took it out and rubbed it over my lips, as if applying a second coat of invisible lip gloss. Then he rubbed it around my chin and eased it back inside my mouth. "Yeah," he kept saying. "You know what I like." I gagged again when he slid more inches of himself inside. "Ooh, your mouth so wet and juicy." He moaned in pleasure, while I continued to moan in pain.

"Ooh, yeah, that's right." He closed his eyes, tilted his head back, and controlled my head movements with his right hand while he kept a handle on the gun in his left. My head was bobbing up and down. I was scared to death, and I wanted this nightmare to be over with.

"Yeah, yeah," he said as he pumped my head even faster on his dick, almost making me choke. With the last push, I felt my teeth cut into his skin. "Aw, bitch!" He slapped me, and I fell backward, blocking his second hit with my free hands. He aimed the gun at me as he backed away and took a moment to examine his hairy dick. "You gon' pay for that one, bitch!" He pushed his hard-on back into his pants, but I could still see the bulge peeking through. "You wanna bite my shit?" He groaned in pain.

Minutes passed before he said another word. I was thinking, *Come on, muthafucka. Do what you came to do and get it over with. On second thought, only if it doesn't involve killing me.*

Where the fuck were those cops, and where in the hell was Sand? It was past three o' clock in the morning. Maybe she was with her girlfriend. Maybe she had moved on without me. Another set of tears came running down. Maybe I should have never come back. I was so confused, and everything at the moment seemed unreal, but I knew that it was. I wondered if Sand still loved me and if she could forgive me. Everything that was happening seemed like karma coming around for the people I had hurt in my life—Sand, Vincent, and Shun. I was stuck, with nowhere to turn. I wished I could change everything, but I couldn't. What was done was done. No turning back.

"Man, where this muthafucka at?" He kept looking at the clock and then again at me. "Bitch, did I ask you to look at me?" He was pacing the floor. Then we heard exactly three knocks on the door. "Bitch, don't fuckin' move."

He walked out of the room, leaving me praying that this would all be over with soon. I heard the door open, and the sound of another male's voice caught my attention.

"Here. Put these on so she can't see you," I heard the guy who had raped me say. I could barely hear the second voice to make out what else was being said.

Then I heard, "Hell no. We agreed on fifty thousand." The rapist was angry. I could pick out his loud, deep voice from anyone else's with no problem at all. "Well, then you finish the job. I've done my part." He was obviously pissed. Sounded like some sort of disagreement. What the hell was going on? I heard the voices get closer and then suddenly disappear.

There were now two men standing in front of my doorway. Both had on all-black clothing, gloves, and black masks. The only way I was able to distinguish the two was by their size and height. The first robber was tall and stocky. The second was shorter and smaller. Were they about to do something so bad to me that he needed a partner? All kinds of crazy shit started running through my mind. Sweat and tears began rolling down my face. I hoped I wasn't about to get a train run on me. I prayed that was not about to happen. I wouldn't be able to go through another round of torture and torment.

"Look at you. So you like to play games with men, huh? Well let's play my game. It's called my secrets, your lies. If you can guess my secret, I'll tell you your lies."

I eyed the new intruder, giving him a blank stare. What was he talking about? What was he thinking? The first guy, the rapist, stood next to the new guy, following along and ready to take action when told. The new guy ran his gloved finger down my cheek. I shivered, frantic at his touch.

"So beautiful, yet so conniving," he said.

What was he talking about? I was scared shitless, and I showed it clearly through the tears that had my eyes burning red and the snot and saliva that drenched my face.

"Man, hurry up," the rapist yelled. I was still balled up, down on the floor. The second masked man stood in front of me, squatted down to be at eye level.

"You go first," he said.

"I'm not sure I understand what you're asking me to do," I said in a low voice, pausing in between my words.

He stood to his feet and started laughing. "Oh, so now you don't understand how to take orders? Well, that's mighty funny." He looked over at the rapist. "You hear that, man? She says she doesn't understand what I want her to do." He laughed again, waiting for his partner to join in, but he didn't.

"Man, we gotta be out. Do what the fuck we came to do, and let's bounce." the rapist said. He extended his hand with the gun to give it to the new guy. He released it, giving the new guy before me all the control.

The new guy waved the weapon in my face, getting a thrill at how I flinched every time he brought it near me. "Any memory of what I'm talking about now?" he asked, showing me a picture of me and Sand. It looked like we were at the mall. *Wait a minute.* We were at the mall. I remembered the outfit. That picture was taken at least six months ago. I remembered the hairdo. I started crying. That was on my birthday. I scrolled down with my eyes, and there was the date and time on the picture. "This is why we couldn't spend time together on your birthday?" he asked.

"Vincent?" I whispered.

"Oh, goddamn, man. Now the bitch knows who you are." The other guy was becoming impatient and angry.

"Oh, my God, Vincent," I said.

Where did he get that picture? We had taken the small photo inside of a picture booth at the Galleria, a shopping mall. I thought back to that day, when I had told Vincent that I was going to be spending time with my grandmother for my birthday. He had really wanted us to be together, but there was no way that I could get away. Sand had been planning my birthday surprise for months. There was just no way in hell she would let me out of her sight. She spent way over five thousand dollars on me that day. I remembered later that night and the fancy four-star hotel we stayed in. I was trying to figure out how Vincent could have gotten the picture. I was sure it was in my photo album, which I kept inside my closet, on the very top shelf. No telling what other pictures he had of me and her.

He looked at the picture again, then ripped it down the middle. "You were all I wanted. I gave my heart to you."

I started crying again, showing him that I was hurt also. I couldn't believe this was the extent to which he would go. I hated him for this. That fat muthafucka behind him had raped me, and it looked like Vincent was the mastermind behind it.

"He raped me!" I yelled in Vincent's face, pointing at the guy standing behind him. All of a sudden my anger took over, and I felt stronger.

"Oh, so he hurt the poor baby? He screwed you like you did me? You lied about everything!" Vincent spat. "Your grandmother, your whereabouts, your entire goddamn life." He became infuriated, but I was just as mad. Now that I knew it was him under that mask, he didn't scare me anymore.

"I'm sorry," was all I could say. Yes I had lied, cheated, and misled him. But he was also wrong. My heart was pumping faster and faster. I had brought all this on myself, and whatever my punishment was, I was ready to take it. But this crazy son of a bitch had me raped and beaten up. "Do I really deserve this, though, Vincent?" Sadness was in my voice. I was trying to understand the bona fide reasoning behind all this.

Vincent snatched the mask off his face and tossed it on the floor. His bright blue eyes looked coal black to me. There was nothing that I could say that would justify the situation, but I wanted to know if Vincent really wanted me killed. If I had hurt him so deeply that his only thought of revenge was for me to die.

"You think I was gonna just let you walk around here like nothing happened between us? You think you can just walk into someone's life and right back out without giving them a goddamn warning? And then you say you're sorry. You weren't sorry when you came over to screw me and then rushed back to lay with your little dyke, now were you?"

I sucked in my own tears. I could see that he was deeply hurt.

"Please, Vincent," I begged. "Don't hurt me. I'm sorry."

"Man, do what the fuck you gotta do so we can bounce," the rapist urged.

Vincent stared me in my face. "It's your turn," he said.

I was still confused. "What?" I cried out.

"Man, you fuckin' takin' too long," the rapist barked. "Give me the gun so I can blow this bitch. She already know who you are—"

Bang!

A loud shot rang out. My ears were ringing, and suddenly I was blinded by a massive amount of blood.

Rene

I sat like a frightened child, with my hands covering my face, my ears ringing from the loud shot that had echoed off the walls of my suddenly silent apartment. The rapist lay facedown in a huge puddle of his own blood, which poured from his head and onto the carpet.

Vincent looked at him and then back at me. "You see what he made me do?"

Now would have been a good time to reach over and slap the shit out of his fat, disgusting ass, then shove my fingers up his rear to see how much he liked it. But while I felt free from the rapist, Vincent still held me captive. My blood was beginning to boil as I predicted my fate. I was sure I was next.

"My God, Vincent. You are crazy!" I shouted.

He started laughing at himself, slapping the gun against his forehead. He had seriously lost his mind.

"It's your turn," he said. I looked up at him, and tears welled up in my eyes. "Tell me my secret!" he screamed loudly, now swinging the gun and aiming it more in my direction.

"I . . . I . . . I don't know. Just tell me, Vincent," I pleaded. "Please don't hurt me."

Just then, we heard a loud bang on my door, and seconds later my bedroom was surrounded by armed police officers, all dressed in black and pointing their weapons directly at Vincent. He looked around as the cops swarmed around him and then back over at me.

"Put the gun down nice and easy, sir," one of the officers instructed, trying to calm him. "Look, this doesn't have to get any uglier than it already is. Just do as I say and put the gun down," he ordered again after noticing Vincent's hesitation.

Vincent continued to watch me as if he and I were still the only ones in the room. "Please, Vincent," I heard my lips beg. "I'm sorry."

Vincent just stood there, as if he was deaf and paralyzed. Then he started to speak.

"When I was five years old, my father would come into my room late at night, while my mother was asleep. 'You awake, Vincent boy?' he would ask me. I would close my eyes tighter, because I already knew what he had come for. Hell, he did it almost every other night. He'd pull my quilt back, slide under there with me, and say he was gonna tell me a bedtime story about a son and his father. He would tell me that a son and his father shared a special bond. And that a son should do whatever a father asked of him when he asked it. If he didn't, he'd be punished. And if he told a soul, the bond would be broken." I saw tears roll down his face, and then he started to cry. "Do you know what my secret is, Rene?"

I looked straight into Vincent's sad eyes and began crying with him. "Yes, Vincent," I said with a sympathetic look. "Yes, I know your secret. He molested you."

He nodded his head, tears streaming down his face like rain. "Rene, I'm sorry." He looked over at the man he had just shot, then at the team of cops, and finally back over at me. "I just wanted you to feel how much hurt and pain I'm in. I didn't mean to hurt you," he confessed. "Please believe me, Rene. I only wanted for you to be happy. It didn't have to come to this. You should have just been honest with me from the start."

As I sat there listening to Vincent pour out his heart to me, I began to feel regret for every lie I had told. I was responsible for everything that had happened tonight, as well as anything that was about to happen. I silently agreed with Vincent that if I had of been honest, it wouldn't have come down to this. I suddenly felt that I loved him. That ounce of feeling that I had in my heart for him had awakened.

"Take care of our baby, Rene. And don't tell her about her daddy." Before I knew it, he was raising the gun to his temple.

"No!" one of the policemen yelled.

Vincent pulled the trigger, and he fell right next to the rapist's lifeless body. Blood splattered in every direction. I was traumatized. My legs were shaking uncontrollably, and so were my hands. One of the officers ran over to me, lifted me up from the floor.

"Here, let's put this around you." He wrapped his jacket around me and walked me out of the room and away from the crime scene.

For about two hours my apartment building was filled with crime-scene detectives and reporters, all of whom I was too shaken up to speak to regarding the shootings.

"Now tell me what happened from start to finish," one of the officers asked me over again.

A female detective had been called out to the scene, but I had refused to say a word to her. "I'm not getting anything out of her," she told the officer who was questioning me now. She walked off, unsatisfied that she had not been able to get a response from me and thus break the case.

I remained quiet. I couldn't believe everything that had just taken place. I felt like I had been dreaming and the whole thing was a terrible nightmare. But it wasn't. I watched as they carried out Vincent's body. Tears came

running down my face once again. *This is all a misun-*
derstanding, I tried to convince myself, knowing it was
really all my fault. I buried my face in my hands. Vincent
had killed himself because of me. I was the reason.

I looked up when one of the officers said, "I've seen
this guy here before. Yeah, he used to steal cars and break
into homes. I've booked him a few times. I think they
called him June Bug. Hell, come to think of it, he lived
right across the street."

"Must've been a lover's quarrel," another officer
chimed in.

I gasped. It couldn't be. I stood up and was able to
identify the man who had raped me as his mask had
been removed. Indeed, it was June Bug from across the
street, his eyes still wide open, as dead as could be. *That*
muthafucka!

They zipped up the bag he was in and rolled him down
the steps. That son of a bitch had raped me.

"He raped me," I cried aloud.

The female detective who had been sent in to talk to
me rushed back over in my direction.

What the hell does she want with me now?

"Miss Brown, I just want to ask you one more question.
Do you know a Cassandra Janene Ross?"

I nodded my head. Damn. Was she that blind? Our picture, as wide as the wall, hung over the fireplace mantel.

"Do you know if she's working for Aundrey Stackson,
now going by the name of James Hill?"

I shook my head. I didn't know what she was talking
about. And what the hell did any of that have to do with
what had happened to me here tonight? All I knew was
that Sand did have a friend by the name of James, but I
couldn't be certain of his last name.

"I'm not sure about that."

"Well, Miss Brown, it seems that your girlfriend is involved with and working for Stackson, who the FBI has been investigating for several years. He's wanted on numerous charges. This is a dangerous man we're talking about here. If this unfolds the way that I am sure it will, you may not be able to see your girlfriend for a long, long time. So are you sure you are unaware of her social dealings with Mr. Stackson?"

Did this damn woman not hear me? "I don't know of him," I said louder than I had intended.

She smiled. "Okay, Miss Brown. Here is my card, and when you are ready to talk to me about what went on tonight, you can reach me. I also wrote down my cell number." I took the card. "You might want to take a look outside before you go out there." She smiled and nodded her head, gesturing for me to take a peek out the blinds.

I walked over to the living room window and glanced down at the large crowd that had assembled. Camera crews were everywhere, along with the inhabitants of the entire apartment complex it seemed. The morning sun was up, and everyone was out trying to see what was going on. I quickly closed the blinds. It definitely wasn't safe to go out there.

She saw the expression on my face. "I can get you out of here easily if you take a ride with me downtown." I looked out the window again. "Straight to the hospital and then down to the station," she offered.

God knows I didn't want my face plastered all over the television.

"They're on live," I heard somebody say.

The female detective walked over, flipped on my television, and there it was.

"We are live here at the scene where two bodies are being carried out of this South Dallas apartment. This homicide-suicide has everyone in awe as they try to piece together what happened here today. Both shootings were witnessed by a young woman who was raped and beaten before these fatal incidents occurred. She told police that one of the two men had somehow gained unauthorized access to her apartment earlier this morning. One of the victims was someone she was involved with. Investigators are working hard to determine the motive for this bizarre attack and are getting little help from the witness involved. We are waiting for more details as they become available. Until then, keep it tuned here. This is Veronica Bradley with Network Four. Back to you, Shannon."

This was déjà vu. I felt like I had been through this whole thing before. I couldn't believe it. I started crying again. Where was Sand? I looked up at the woman detective, who was watching my every move. She handed me a brown paper bag.

"Go in the bathroom and change," she said.

I looked in the bag and saw a pair of joggers, a T-shirt, a wig, and some shades. I had no choice. I went into the bathroom, emptied the bag of its contents, and tried to change my appearance as much as I could. After I slipped on the hideous blond wig, my look changed drastically. I was in full disguise. I didn't even know who I was.

When I came out of the bathroom, the detective was talking to one of the forensic guys working the crime scene. After she spotted me, she waved me over to join them.

"Rene, we need to talk." She raised a ziplock bag, and inside was a small gold hoop earring and a small black tape. "Does this belong to you?"

I shook my head no.

Hours later I was down at the police station, being asked all kinds of questions, like I was a suspect. They had me all hemmed in, in a small-ass room, waiting for someone else to come in and ask me the same damn questions that the first detective had asked. I had my hands folded, and I was leaned back in my seat, waiting impatiently for them to finish this nonsense so that I could leave.

The room was freezing cold, and other than the armed security guard and I, it held no life or warmth. Just a tiny, confined space designed to make people go crazy so that they could tell all they knew. I looked over to my left, at the officer that was watching me closely. This was the kind of shit that I had seen on television. I had never thought it would happen to me. I wished they would hurry the hell up so I could go somewhere, anywhere, and take a shower. I'd bathe in the Trinity River if they'd let me go right now. That was how desperately I needed to wash that asshole's funk juice off of me. The odor taunted my nostrils, and every time I inhaled, I felt the urge to vomit.

I was startled when a tall, young white boy, entered the room. He had on a gray suit, with a crisp white shirt underneath. He walked over, unfolded the brown fold-up chair, then took a seat beside me. He placed his briefcase before him and began shuffling through several folders.

"How you doing there? I'm Detective Rockwall."

I looked up at him with an attitude.

He went on. "I know you've already spoken with Detective Lochardt, but I wanted to go over a few more things with you. They brought me in here to fill in because I'm also working on the Turner case, and at this point, we see a connection."

"What Turner case?"

He retrieved a thick brown folder from the bottom of his pile. It was stuffed with so many papers that they slid out as soon as he opened it. "If you know any of these people that I am about to show you, I need to know."

I didn't understand why I was being interrogated. I was the damn victim here, and here they were, treating me like this.

He pulled out a five-by-seven mug shot. "Do you happen to know him?" I picked up the picture and looked at it carefully.

"Never seen him," I said.

"Okay." He took the picture out of my hand and laid it to the side, facedown. "What about this picture?"

I glanced at it the same way I had the first one. "Never seen her, either."

"Last but not least." He waved another photo in my face.

"Oh my God."

"What, Miss Brown? Do you recognize the person in the picture?"

I couldn't believe my eyes. I covered my mouth with my hands. "That's . . . that's my girlfriend."

The detective pulled the picture away and stood up from his seat. "Miss Brown, do you know how much trouble your girlfriend is in right now?"

I shook my head.

"Let's just say enough trouble where she may never see daylight again."

I couldn't believe what I was hearing. This man had to be putting me on. What the fuck was he talking about? I still wasn't sure.

"What is all this about?" I asked.

"We were able to retrieve a few good prints from your apartment. We entered them into our database and found a match. We can place your girlfriend at the murder scene of Jasmine Keshawn Turner, the nineteen-year-old woman killed in her Fort Worth home."

I was in shock. My eyes widened, and my body grew stiff. What was he implying? This couldn't be happening.

He saw the look in my eyes. "I know this seems a little unreal, but we have hard proof and a witness who says she saw your girlfriend visit Ms. Turner on more than one occasion. We also have obtained phone records of inbound and outbound calls placed between Cassandra and Jasmine. We were also able to get a statement from a friend of Jasmine's that says she witnessed phone arguments between the two on several occasions."

"What!"

"With the evidence that I have now, it's enough to go after her."

I looked at him as if to ask, "Are you kidding me?" There was just no way in hell. I bit down on my lip to keep from crying. *Murder,* I kept repeating in my head. He had said he had enough evidence to pin Sand with murder. "But . . ." *Oh hell, what is coming now?*

He looked over at the guard and then leaned in toward me and practically whispered, "After reviewing the case and seeing that your girlfriend has no previous record and basically a clean slate, I found it kind of hard to believe myself. So that's when I decided to dig a little deeper. We followed Cassandra for a couple of days, and nothing she did was out of habit, except for one thing. She purchased a nine-millimeter pistol."

My eyes grew even wider. Sand ain't never had a gun. Hell nah. He didn't have his facts straight. I had to speak up. "Sand don't even like guns," I protested.

"Well, that may be true, but I was able to get a copy of the receipt and a tape from the surveillance camera from the store where she purchased it."

"Oh my God," I replied in disbelief.

"I know this sounds like a lot to take in right now, but what I need from you is to think back to anyone she may know who would want to frame her, because as of right now she is a prime suspect." He handed me a sheet of clean notebook paper. I looked at the blank sheet but was not able to think of any names, because I didn't know any of her friends. Sand had never introduced me to anyone. He waited.

I finally spoke. "Detective Rockwall, I can't help you." Although it seemed like he was a decent cop and it sounded like he was on our side, the truth was, I didn't have a clue who Sand's friends were and where she hung out. I really didn't know anything about her. Everything was a secret. Plus, I hadn't had time to keep up with what was going on in Sand's life, because I had been too busy trying to hide the mess going on in mine.

"Okay. I'm just going to have to use my outside sources. You find somewhere to stay for the next few nights. I don't think it's safe for you to go back home." He looked very sincere.

"Okay. Can I go now?"

He handed me a card and wrote in his cell and his direct office number. "If you hear from Sand or if you can remember anything, I need you to give me a call. It's best you deal with me and only me."

I took the card and slipped it into my wallet. "Okay."

I stood up and walked out. As soon as I turned the corner, I pulled out my cell and dialed Shun's number. I couldn't wait to hear from my friend again. She answered on the first ring.

"Hello. This is Miss Shun. And who is this interrupting my Popeyes chicken dinner?"

"Shun!" I cried. "I need you to come get me."

"Rene?"

"Yes. I'm at the downtown police station."

"What! Don't worry. I'll be right there. Hang tight."

"Okay," I said, relieved.

I waited outside the headquarters, on a hard cement bench, in the nippy wind, watching people entering and leaving the station. Sand was in some deep shit, and I needed to find her. I tried calling her cell again. Still no answer. I kept trying.

About forty-five minutes later Shun made it to the station. I stood up quickly when I heard her loud-ass muffler screaming. She was in that old-ass faded blue Cutlass that one of her baby daddies had left her with. I walked toward the car and then tried to get in on the passenger side.

"Unlock the door," I yelled through the glass.

She put her eyeglasses on and then rolled down the window. "Rene?"

"Yeah, it's me. Open the door. It's cold out here.

She unlocked the door hesitantly, and I hopped in. She stared at me with a confused look on her face, acting like she ain't never seen nobody in a blond-ass, crooked wig before.

"Girl, I almost didn't know who you was, sitting on that bench in that white girl wig, looking like a Harry Hines two-dollar hooker. I was just saying to myself, 'That's one bold-ass hooker to be tricking right in front of the police station.'" Shun was laughing her head off at me and the way the blond wig had tilted itself to the side of my head. She saw that I was in no mood for jokes and quickly erased the funny face. "Aw, what's wrong, baby? You don't look too good. What happened to you?" She touched my forehead with the back of her hand, checking for a temperature.

I couldn't hold them back any longer. The more I tried, the more I felt a migraine coming on. I broke down in tears. Shun pulled into a fast-food parking lot a few blocks up from the station and stopped the car. She turned off the ignition and faced me.

"What's wrong, Rene? Talk to me."

I raised my head up and pulled off the ridiculous wig. "Shun, he's dead," I said in a muffled voice.

"Who's dead?"

I got quiet for a moment. Then I said, "Vincent."

She looked at me with surprise and doubt in her eyes. "What!"

I continued to cry, somehow managing to tell her everything that had happened. She couldn't believe it her damn self.

"June Bug raped you?"

I nodded my head, too embarrassed and humiliated to tell her the whole truth behind it. And for some horrible reason, I felt like I had brought it all on myself.

Shun was in shock. She leaned over to hug me. "I'm sorry, Rene. I should have been there for you." She squeezed me tighter. "I'm so sorry, baby." She brushed my hair with her hands, gently rubbed the side of my face with the tips of her fingers, and calmed me. It was the softest touch a female could offer. Then out of nowhere, she leaned in a little bit more, lifted my chin, and before I could blink, her lips were softly touching mine.

Sand

The van barely missed me. I quickly swerved and ran up on a curb and into a fire hydrant. "Fuck!" I yelled, angry at whoever it was that couldn't read the goddamn yield sign. I knew from the impact that Ms. Lady was definitely bruised. I backed the car up, pulled off the service road and into a half-empty car lot. I opened my car door, got out, and walked around the front of the car to view the damage.

"Are you okay, son?" an elderly woman asked when she saw me get out of the car. She and her friend with her had seen the whole thing.

"Yes, ma'am, I'm all right."

"I tell ya one thing. People can't drive no more like they used to. I'm just glad they missed ya, or that would have been an ugly wreck." Grandma looked like she was pushing ninety, and so did her friend, and they were actually shopping around for vehicles. That shit had to be against the law. They walked off, going back to what they were doing.

Ms. Lady was all right, despite the dent and the new paint job I was going to have to give her. She was still drivable. I wondered why so much shit had been happening to me lately. Was this God's way of punishing me for something I did? I hopped back in my car and drove out of the car lot. I looked in the rearview and took in the stares of those who watched me as I drove away. I didn't know where I was headed, but my pedal was damn near all the way down to the floor. I was mad as hell. Images of Rene flashed through my mind as I remembered once again what Shun had told me. I punched the steering wheel with my fist several times like a maniac. I couldn't believe Rene. She had a baby with some man. I had thought she loved me and only me.

Screech!

I made a quick, sharp turn. *Fuck going home.* I needed to get away. I didn't know where I was going, but I was going. I had so much shit running through my mind that I could not think straight. She fucked off on me, I thought. Even though I had cheated on her with Jasmine on more than one occasion, I still felt that her fucking off was the ultimate betrayal. She hadn't wanted for a muthafuckin' thing. And this was how she repaid me? "This is the thanks I get?" I hollered. Over and over again, I thought back to how I would call her cell and not be able to reach her. I thought back to how she had come home with hickeys and shit, lying by saying they were mosquito bites. I recalled the numerous occasions when she had come home and I would go down on her like the shit was all mine. How wrong had I been? I wanted to fuckin' throw up.

Just wait till I see that bitch. She got me fucked up.

I was in la-la land by the time the young bartender poured me another drink. I was posted up on a bar stool, downing the last of six glasses of vodka. I was tossing them back-to-back, straight to the head, no sip-sip shit. I gave him a hundred-dollar bill to go on top of that shelf of theirs and pull me down some liquor.

"You gonna be all right there, buddy?"

"Yeah, I'm straight." I tried sliding myself off the stool—first the right foot and then the left.

Boom!

I hit the floor. He rushed over to grab me and pull me up to my feet, but he was unsuccessful. "Damn, man, you gonna get me fired. We just got this place. My pops is gonna kill me if he finds out I gave you that much to drink. You know, we could lose our license." I was in a daze. I could hardly hear or see. "Man, we gotta get you home. I can't let you leave like this. What's your name, buddy? You got a name? Is there anybody that can come pick ya up? Huh?"

"My name Sssss."

"What's that?"

"Cccaasssandra."

"Cassandra? Wait a minute. You's a woman?" He laughed. "You're shitting me. So, uh, you one of them there butchos? Cool. I ain't never seen no black girl butcho, 'specially being over here in this hick town and all. I thought only us had that problem." He started laughing some more. I was still on the floor, helpless. "Damn, you could've fooled me." I could feel him bring me to my feet and then slide me into a booth. He laid me down and stretched my feet out.

He went on. "Now, I'm gonna go through your wallet and see if I can find somebody to come get you. My dad won't be gone long." I felt him slide his hand into my pocket. "I'm going through your wallet right now. I'm not stealing your money. I'm grabbing a card out. It says, 'Nessa, barber and beautician.'"

I nodded my head and groaned so he could see me.

"Okay, I'll call her." It was quiet, and then I heard him punching in numbers on a phone. "Hello. May I speak to Nessa? Nessa, hi. This is Jim. I have a friend of yours here at my bar, and she, or I mean he, won't be able to drive tonight. Cassandra, I believe, is the name." I heard the young bartender pause for a minute. "You want to know how his hair is? Uh, okay. It's braided back. It's long, and there are some cool-looking white beads hangin' on the ends. Yes, it's been a couple of hours. Yes. Okay. You exit at Keller Springs and make a right. Go down until you see the little redbrick building that says Big Jim's Place. Okay. I'll tell him, I mean, her."

Click.

"Hey, your friend Nessa say she gonna send a friend to come and get you. Just hang tight. If my pops gets here, you staggered in like this, okay?"

I nodded my head.

"We just gon' have to come back for your car tomorrow." Deja was buckling me up on the passenger side of her car. My head hurt like hell. "What in the hell are you doing way over here on this hillbilly side of town, anyway?" I had no clue myself. My head was still pounding. "Sand, tell me what's wrong with you." She grabbed my chin and was staring into my eyes for an answer. "I'm here for you. If you would just talk to me."

I turned my head, and her hand fell into her lap.

"What? It's something you don't wanna talk to me about? I understand. It's your woman's job to comfort you."

I looked back at her. There was so much I wanted to tell her. So much that I needed to get off my chest but couldn't. Deja was stepping into my life at the wrong time. I couldn't bring her into all this. She turned her head away and looked out the other window. Suddenly, the quietness stole the moment, and she didn't have anything else to say. I sat there for the long drive, thankful she had come to my rescue once again. There was something different about Deja. She had a sensitive side that made me feel comfortable around her, even though I had known her only for a short time. The silence was broken when she asked if I had heard about what happened today.

"You know, they found two guys dead in those Sunridge Apartments in South Dallas. They had broken into this woman's house and raped her. One shot the other, and the other shot himself. That's a damn shame. They wouldn't show the girl's face, but I hope it ain't nobody I know."

At that moment it hit me. "That's where I live," I struggled to say. My mind raced back to Rene. "Deja, I need to get home." Suddenly, I saw red and blue lights flashing in her eyes. She looked in the rearview mirror, and I turned around to look behind us.

"Goddamn. What now?" she muttered. She rolled to a stop on the side of the road and rolled down her window.

I sat up as straight as I could, and in my mouth I popped a green apple Jolly Rancher candy that she had lying in her cup holder. I tried to pat the wrinkles out of my pants, but it wasn't working. I had sobered up a little, but not enough.

"Driver, turn off the engine and slowly step out of the car."

"What? What the hell I do?" Deja screamed out the window. "I have my license and registration."

"Deja, just kill the engine," I warned her.

"But, Sand, why I gotta get out the car? We out here in the middle of nowhere, and they askin' me to get out the car."

"I don't know. Just be cool and do what they say. It's cool."

She turned off the engine and slowly opened her car door. I looked back, and two black officers were standing near their patrol car, with guns pointed our way. This shit didn't feel right. We hadn't violated any traffic laws.

"Now spread your legs and place your hands on the roof of the car."

I saw Deja doing as she was told. She was watching me through the glass with fear in her eyes. Her mascara ran down her cheeks.

"Passenger, step out of the vehicle, spread your legs apart, and place both your hands on the roof of the car."

I slowly opened the door just enough to ease out. *What the hell is going on?* I knew this was no ordinary traffic stop, but I did as I was told. It was dark out, a Sunday night, and very few people passed us by. I was facing Deja. Her bottom lip was trembling.

One of the cops made his way over to me, and the other stood back, waiting to take action. "Are you Cassandra Janene Ross?" he asked.

"Yeah, that's me."

"I'm placing you under arrest for the murder of Jasmine Keshawn Turner." He forced my hands behind my back and snapped on some tight handcuffs. Deja just looked at me, trying to figure out what was going on.

"Man, I ain't killed nobody," I said.

He slammed my head on the car, proceeded to pat me down, and read me my rights.

"You have the right to remain silent—"

"Man, this is some bullshit!" I glanced at Deja, and tears were racing down her face. "Deja, I ain't kill nobody," I yelled out. I wanted her to believe me.

The officer shoved me into the backseat of his Crown Victoria. Deja just shook her head.

"Man, I said I ain't kill nobody," I yelled to the other officer, who was strapping up his seat belt in the driver's seat. The officer who had manhandled me jumped in the backseat with me.

The officer who was driving pulled up alongside Deja's car. "You have a nice night, young lady, and drive safe," he said before pulling away and back onto the road.

I looked behind me, and Deja was still watching me, crying and not understanding the shit that had just happened. "I ain't killed nobody," I said over and over.

"Here. Give her this." The driver passed something back to the officer next to me.

"Yeah, you gon' like this." He raised his hand and showed me a long-ass needle. I tried to back away, but it was useless, because I had nowhere to turn. "Go to sleep, little baby. Go to sleep," he sang.

And then I felt a flutter of coldness being injected into my arm. My eyes felt heavy. My high had returned. Seconds later I was fast asleep.

I felt a cold breeze tap me on my shoulders. I could barely turn my neck around because it hurt so bad. I had no idea where I was, but I knew for damn sure it wasn't at home. I was trying to remember if I had once again drunk too many drinks and maybe followed some female home. The more I widened my eyes and sucked in dirty air, the more I regained consciousness. My eyes roamed around the room in every direction as I lay on my back, wondering how the hell I had got here. I tried to sit up, but both my arms were tied tight to a bedpost. I looked toward my feet. They were also tied down and spread far apart. I had no idea how I had gotten here. I tried pulling my arms out of the ropes, but it was no use. They weren't budging, and pulling only made the red marks around my wrists darker.

"Who the fuck is in here?" I hollered as loud as I could. I heard nothing. Then I saw the door slowly open and a female appear in the doorway. She was completely naked except for a pair of long, black, shiny boots. She eased her way in my direction. As she got closer, I knew exactly who I was dealing with—Chyna. She stepped onto the bed where I lay. Her long black boots were dangerously close to my face, daring me to move so that I could get stepped on. Once she was standing directly over me, she squatted down.

"Have you thought about what we talked about?"

I looked at her like she was crazy. If she was talking about that little proposal she had offered me, she could forget it. I wasn't about to do a damn thing with keeping track of who was selling the most pussy or trickin' no ho off. That wasn't my style. I rolled my eyes.

"So is that a no?"

I turned my head. *So is this what this is all about?* I thought. *All of this?*

She stood up again. "You know, Sand, I don't like to be told no." She made a smirking sound. "In fact, I have never been told no." She grinned and then quickly erased the expression. "I've always gotten what I wanted when I wanted. So you know that you're making this harder than what it should be? I make you a perfectly nice offer to become a part of a million-dollar network and you turn me down?" She looked me dead in the face, but Chyna didn't scare me. She was just another bitch who wanted to be in control of something.

"Chyna, we might as well get this over with, because I don't have any good news for you. I ain't gonna do it, and that's that."

"Humph. Oh, really?" She rose up slowly, and I caught a glimpse of her trim midsection. "Well, let's see if this changes your mind. Let her in!" She turned her head to face the door. Another naked body appeared before me. She was one of the strippers from the graduation party. I remembered her performance very well. She handed Chyna a long pair of orange scissors.

What was she about to do to me?

Chyna took the scissors in her hand and brought them down to my face, then lowered them toward my middle. She began cutting my jeans off, along with my boxers. "You like this, huh? You like this?" She ripped the clothing from underneath me and tossed it to the floor. She ran her hands over my split and then up again to my stomach. I cringed. The other girl pulled her hair up into a loose bun, and before I knew it, her warm lips and tongue had taken a dive between my legs. I yanked and turned, then squeezed my legs together as tight as I could to keep the girl from coming near my area. My yells and screams didn't matter at all.

Chyna cackled like an evil witch. She looked at me and said, "All the pussies in this house, I own, including yours. I got a video ready to roll. The cover'll read *Dyke Butch Gets Dicked*." I was still fighting with the ropes and yelling for them to rise up. Chyna started laughing and had a crooked smile of satisfaction on her face. "What? You ain't never had the kitty played with before?" She motioned to the stripper. "Fantasy, do your thing, doll." Chyna walked to the foot of the bed and took a front-row seat. Next thing I knew, Fantasy's fingers were inching inside of me. "How you like it, Mama? Three fingers or four?"

Rene

"Shun, what the hell are you doing?" I pushed her off of me. She pulled away and turned her head in the opposite direction, as if she couldn't stand to look me in the face.

"I'm sorry," she said quickly. "Forget that happened. I was just having a moment."

I was blown away. My best friend had just tried to swallow my ass down her long, deep throat, and now she was asking me to forget it had even happened. Oh, hell no. We had some talking to do. This was not the Shun whom I knew. Not the Shun who believed if you kissed someone from the same sex, other than your mama or a child, you would be condemned. This was not the Shun who lived by the "strictly dickly" saying and would add that she had four kids to prove that she loved dick too much ever to convert to some coochie. Evidently, Shun had some things she needed to get off her chest. *What the hell's going on?*

I grabbed her by the arm. "Shun, talk to me, damn it! It's me, Rene," I said, pointing to my chest. "Tell me what's going on with you."

She looked over my shoulder at the car parked beside us, which seemed to be having some sort of car trouble. They had been in the same spot before we pulled in.

"Rene, you are so lucky. You're beautiful, smart, and you can have anything you want. I look at you, and I hate to admit it, but I wish my life could be like yours. I wish I had somebody to take care of me like Sand does you. I wish I had a man that wanted to marry me and be with me for the rest of his life. I wish I could walk down the street and turn heads the way you do." Tears dropped from her eyes. "But I can't. I can see why Sand loves you so much. I never really hated Sand. I just wanted what you had, and that was love."

I was surprised. I looked Shun in the face and wondered if she was putting on one of her acts. I just couldn't believe her confession. I didn't know the appropriate response or reaction, so I let her continue to talk, and I sat there and listened while she opened up and poured out her heart.

Shun and I talked all the way back to her house. She shared a lot, and in a way, I was glad that she did. I didn't know why she felt like she couldn't have come to me sooner. I would have listened. After all, that was what friends were for. I blamed myself for not figuring it out any sooner. The truth was, Shun hated her own life. Her unhappiness was what made her view of things seem so irrational. All she wanted and needed was someone to love her so that she could love them back.

She admitted to me that she had told Sand all about me, Vincent, and the baby, out of anger. I was mad as hell after that. I knew that Sand would have nothing to do with me now. I tried calling her cell phone, and still it rang continuously, with no answer. I called our house, and there was still no answer or messages. I had no idea where she could be. For all I knew, she was laid up under that skeezer, trying to pay me back for fucking off on her. She would never forgive me. I had crossed the line, and there was no turning back.

Days later . . .
"Detective Rockwall speaking." His voice sounded much deeper over the phone.

"Yes, hi, Detective. This is Rene Brown. I was calling to see if you had any new leads on the Turner case."

"Aww, yes, Miss Brown. I was hoping to hear from you. I have learned some very interesting information, and I would like to meet with you again to go over what I have. Is there a way we can meet somewhere in private?"

I thought for a minute. I would have invited him to Shun's, where I was, but with the kids hollering at each other all the time, I knew we wouldn't be able to understand a word the other was saying. Instead, I asked if we could meet at the pizza parlor right around the corner. He agreed. I gave him directions, and we ended the call.

As I waited for Mr. Rockwall at the pizza parlor, I went ahead and ordered a meet lover's pizza with a couple of slices of garlic toast and a strawberry soda. I was hungry as hell. I hadn't eaten anything all day, and it was going on seven thirty. The sun had gone down, and the restaurant was unusually crowded for a Wednesday night. I was wearing some of Shun's old rags, so I hoped Detective Rockwall would recognize me. I had on some ugly green tights that sagged on me and a long T-shirt that covered me like a nightgown.

I spotted the detective the moment he stepped foot inside the place. He was carrying a black briefcase at his side. He started in my direction. I was in the very back, seated near a window.

"I was hoping you hadn't gotten lost." I moved the pizza box over to the booth directly behind me since no one was sitting there. He sat down across from me, checking out his surroundings.

"Hey there. Let's make this quick," he said. I noticed that he seemed extremely nervous, and every time someone passed by, he would look in another direction, like he was paranoid that they would hear us. He flipped open his briefcase. "We got us a situation." He took another glance around. "We have some dirty uniforms, and from what I've heard, it's not just a handful that I can pick out. The department is flooded with them. Right now the only person who I can trust, and who knows that I'm here with you right now, is my partner, Detective Lochardt." He removed a small ziplock bag from his briefcase, along with records and folders. "You see this earring?"

I looked at it closely. It was the same gold hoop earring I remembered Detective Lochardt asking me about. I nodded my head.

"This earring belonged to Jasmine Keshawn Turner, the victim in a homicide a few days ago. This earring was found in your apartment. Now, from the way it looks, Jasmine was murdered in her home." He looked up to make sure I was following him, and so far I was. "Uh-uh. She was not murdered in her home. She was murdered in *yours*." He paused, and I almost fell off my chair.

"What!"

"I know it may sound crazy, but someone murdered her in your home, cleaned the scene, then took her body back to her apartment, and staged the scene to make it look as if she had been murdered there. Jasmine's autopsy report also confirms that the cause of death was not what was reported. She died from a fatal blow to the back of the head, and not from suffocation or strangulation. The police report said that there was forced entry and that they found her with a pillowcase over her head. Although that is what's in all the reports, my gut tells me that's not what happened. Someone is protecting the *real* killer."

Now I was lost, and he could tell by the look on my face. "What the hell was she doing in my apartment?" I asked him.

"Apparently, she and Cassandra were quite an item, according to Spliff. You do know Spliff, don't you?"

I shook my head. Lying through my teeth. I placed a hand on my temple. This was a lot to take in.

"So, now the question remains, if Sand didn't kill Jasmine, who did?"

"I don't know. But I know Sand didn't have anything to do with it." That was my cue to get the hell up out of there. "I'm sorry, Detective, but I have to get going." I pushed my chair back, grabbed my purse, and practically hopped out of my seat.

"Rene!"

I stopped in my tracks and turned back in his direction.

"Be careful!"

I was back at Shun's house, watching her shampoo her hair in the kitchen sink. "Did you hear what I said, Shun?"

"I hear you. Pass me that towel."

"So what you think? I mean, there's just no way."

"Let them figure the shit out. That's their job," she hollered. She towel dried her hair and watched me as I sat in one of her dining room chairs, puzzled, picking my brain.

"Something just ain't adding up," I told her.

I grabbed the cordless receiver and punched in Sand's cell phone number. Still no answer. I had been unsuccessful at trying to reach her by phone. Maybe she had tried calling me. I entered in my own missing cell phone number to check for messages of any kind. It rang, and a woman's voice completely caught me off guard.

"Sand can't talk right now. She's a little tied up." *Click!*

Sand

Chyna walked around the room, holding a bat that sort of looked like the one I owned. In fact, it was exactly like mine. "So, you wanna be stubborn? Sand, I can make your life a living hell. Don't you know that by now? The police are already looking for you. Do you know how much power I have and what the fuck I can do to you? I make muthafuckas disappear off the face of the earth without a trace. I make niggas and hoes lay it down. I'm the bitch running this show. Now, if you don't wanna get down, I'm gonna have to gon' and knock ya down."

I spit out the blood that had filled my mouth. They had already raped me. Now she wanted to torture and beat me to death. She took another home-run swing at my face.

"Owww!" I yelled. I felt like my jaw had been crushed.

"Aw, did I hurt the poor baby?" This bitch was psychotic. She lifted the bat again, for the third time. I closed my eyes and tightened my body, bracing myself for the pain I knew was sure to come.

Splat! She slammed the bat hard across my belly. I tried to break away, but I was still tied down. She laughed at herself and the marks she had made.

"Damn, my nigga. You fucked up." She walked around the room, tapping the bat on the floor, watching me howl in pain. "You know, that girlfriend of yours is a sneaky bitch, huh?" She stopped in her tracks to look back down at me.

What the fuck is she talking about?

"If only she had been home that day, I wouldn't have had to try to cover my tracks," she said, nearly out of breath.

How is Rene in this? I continued to lie there, helpless and in so much damn pain.

"If she had been there that night," she continued, "we could have leveled things out, and this shit would have been over by now. And that other bitch wouldn't be six feet under right now."

My eyes popped open, because I knew she was referring to Jasmine.

She threw the bat in my direction, barely missing my head, and pulled out a sharp-ass blade.

"Chyna, you ain't gotta do this shit, man," I pleaded. "That girl didn't mean shit to me," I admitted.

I didn't know what Chyna was about to do to me. She climbed back onto the bed and ran her fingers up and down my blistered arms. I flinched with every shaky move. Her eyes were staring at the picture on my arm. She appeared to be admiring the mini-portrait of Rene. She brought the blade near my arms and pretended to be outlining the tattoo.

"No, no, no. Don't do this, man."

She chuckled. "I'm not gonna cut your punk ass. I was just picturing your bitch with that same smile on her face after I rip her ass apart."

"Come on, Chyna. All the work I pushed for you. Come on. Please leave Rene out of this," I begged. Although I was still mad at Rene for everything she had done, I couldn't allow her to pay for my mistakes. I still loved her; that other shit could be dealt with later. I finally gave in. "Whatever you need me to do, I'll do it. Just don't fuck with my girl."

Saying that brought me relief. She smiled a wicked smile. "That's what I'm talking about. Now, you see, that's all you had to do from the start." She hopped off the bed and walked out the door, slamming it behind her. "Fletch," I heard her say. "Untie the bitch. She finally givin' me some act right."

Moments later, the door slowly crept back open. I thought maybe it was Fletch coming in to finish me off. I thought maybe the offer, my life in exchange for Rene's, was no longer on the table. But it wasn't Fletch creeping in; it was Peaches. *What the hell is she doing here?* But then I remembered she worked for Chyna. Therefore, this was her home.

She ran in, watching her back. "Shhh . . . shhh." She had a towel in one hand and a bottle of water in the other. She poured a little water on the towel and proceeded to wipe the bloody areas of my face. I moaned. "Shhh. I know it hurts." Tears sneaked from my eyes. "Come on, Sand. Don't break, baby. Don't break. They're just testing you."

"What do they want from me?" I asked.

She looked behind her once again, checking to be sure no one could hear us. She whispered, "If I tell you that, they'll kill me." She looked sincere.

"Please," I begged. "Tell me."

"You know Chyna got hoes out the ass working for her, right?"

I nodded my head.

"Well, it ain't what ya think. Forget all that shit you think you know. Those hoes working the corners are just cover-ups for what really goes down. The real bitches out working, they ain't prostituting and tricking her pussy on the streets. There's a separate clientele that they serve—the rich and the famous."

I didn't understand.

Peaches went on. "Yeah, that's right. Filthy rich white folks. And ain't nothing like some black pussy with white stuff all on her."

She stood up, propped her left leg on the bed for balance, and stuffed her fingers inside her vagina. She pulled out what looked like a long, thick glass test tube. It was filled with white powder. "Chyna goes to the extreme with the shit," she said. "You get the bitch and the high for a nice price. The finer the bitch, the more she has to offer, and the more she costs."

I was in shock. I wondered if Peaches was telling me the truth, but she had the evidence right in front of me.

"I know you probably wondering how I got down with all this, but I'm gon' tell you now. You don't find Chyna. Chyna finds you." She shoved the glass test tube back in her womanhood like it was a tampon and pulled her skirt back down.

"Well, what category do you fall in?" I asked, still aching from the pain.

"Pttt, there isn't one for me. I'm just on the payroll."

When she said that, my doubts about Peaches resurfaced. It was still possible that she was a part of this mess. I just couldn't figure out how. Right now, I couldn't trust anyone, including her ass.

"Sand, this ain't about you. It was never about you. You just kinda got caught in the middle." That was too hard to believe. She smiled, wiped my face once again, and left the room.

I was dealing with devils here. And if they wanted to dance, they picked the wrong nigga.

Rene

It has been three months and two days since I had been raped. I still had not been able to get Sand off my mind or Vincent. On top of that, Detective Rockwall, who had been trying to help me find Sand, had been found shot to death in a motel room, and all of his case files were missing. I had tried calling his partner, but she no longer worked there. To make matters worse, the new detective who had replaced her acted like she had no idea what I was even talking about. I had asked her about the girl Jasmine who was found dead in her townhome three months ago, and she had told me that the name Jasmine Turner didn't even ring a bell. I had gone down to the police station to try to get some information in person, and they'd thought I was going crazy.

Obviously, the police would be no help, so I did a little research on my own. There was no death certificate for Jasmine Keshawn Turner. And when I tried to pull up something on her, I got the screen messages no match found and unable to locate. It was like her entire identity had disappeared, like the shit had never even happened.

Next, I tried pulling up Sand's name in the phone book, and nothing came up. I searched through every public record book I could find, and still there was nothing that would lead me to her. It was like she had vanished, ceased to exist.

I just didn't understand how my life had got shattered in the blink of an eye. I had been staying with Shun since everything had happened. I knew I was getting on her nerves, pestering her with my problems and worries.

A few days later, my prayers were answered when I received a package in the mail addressed to my eyes only. I hoped it was something from Sand, letting me know she was okay and that she forgave me. I tore at the box, ripping it open as quickly as I could with my bare hands. I dumped everything onto the floor. I picked up an envelope, which had fallen out first. Inside was a letter. I didn't understand it. It was the exact same letter I had written to Sand. Why would she send me a letter I had written? I flipped it over to look at the back.

> *Rene,*
> *If you're reading this, that means you're okay and in a safe place and I am in trouble somewhere. I will not go into details, because I'm not sure this package has reached you. Call the phone number on the box, and she will tell you everything you need to know. Please trust me.*
> *Still love you,*
> *Sand*

I looked on the box, and there was no phone number or return address. There was no postage tracking or anything. I flipped the box over, examining it carefully. What number was she talking about? I looked closer. The fake UPC code was the telephone number. I dashed for the telephone, then dialed the number as quick as I could. A woman answered on the first ring.

"So you received my package?"

"Hello. This is Rene, Sand's girlfriend. Is something wrong? Where is she?" I asked, crying.

"Hello, Rene. I've been anticipating your call. I assure you your girlfriend is fine, just out putting in a little work for me, you could say. But let me just cut to the chase. You know something very valuable and helpful that could keep you and your girlfriend alive."

What is she talking about?

"All I'm gonna say is this. Meet me tonight, and we can discuss the details."

"I'm sorry, but I don't know what you're talking about. And who are you? You must have me confused with someone else."

"Oh, no I don't. I'll give you a little background about yourself. Let's see. You worked for Albery Johnson at Johnson and Johnson law firm. You were the receptionist and an underpaid accountant there, although you may have thought that chump change he was paying you was something compared to the other underpaid legal team. I know that you were also in charge of bank deposits, transfers, and withdrawals."

My face lit up, and my mouth fell open in shock. *Where is this bitch going with this?*

"I also know that before you left, you snuck a piece of the action. Or do you prefer 'borrowed it from petty cash'? Hell, I would have done the same thing too, particularly knowing what we both know he was doing to the poor black folk—overcharging us and selling our cases. Now, is that enough research on somebody to say you know them?"

I was quiet and was feeling as though she had too much info on me. Where the hell did she come from, and what problem did she have with me? I had no idea that what I had done so long ago would catch up with me now, especially like this, and from some stranger.

"Now, Rene, I know you are a smart girl, and I know you love Sand. So give me the information I need, and you both can go on with your precious little lives."

"What if I don't have what you're looking for?"

"Don't worry. You do. Call me when you're ready to talk about a meeting place." *Click!* She hung up just like that.

Oh, my God. Who is that bitch, and what does she want from me? I racked my brain, trying to figure it out. Then I came up with only one reason—the Wilson case. It was the only case that Albery had ever lost in his career as a defense attorney. That case had stirred up more mess in Dallas than CNN could ever broadcast. According to rumors, Albery was paid millions of dollars to lose that case, but I had tried not to get involved in any of that. I had done what I was paid to do—answer phones, make deposits, withdrawals, and transfers. I might have sneaked a little under the table, but it was one time and one time only. *Shit.* What was ten grand to someone who made triple that amount in his sleep?

Epilogue

"Yeah, I have to up the price a little tonight," Sand said. The caller on the line didn't give a damn. He had bought products from Chyna before, and he was what you called a satisfied customer. He always came back for more. Money was no object for him. "How many you want in there?"

"Uh, surprise me, damn it. My plane just touched down, and I'm horny as fuck. I need to show my man Jermaine here a real good time here in Dallas tonight."

"I see, I see. Well, you know I'll make your stay here in the D well worth it. I'll put you down for the duo special. What color you like tonight? White on black or white on white?"

"I'm feeling a little naughty tonight. Let us have both."

"All right. That'll be five grand apiece."

"No problem. I'm wiring the money as we speak."

Sand hit the disconnect button and jotted down quick notes in code on her laptop.

G-man arrival 2:00 a.m. Duo special, 5k per girl, buddy come along + pleasure pkg. 6911.

She clicked on the Internet icon to see if the money had reached the account before she sent the e-mail to both Sabrina's and Angel's cell. The money was there. Everything was set. She looked over her shoulder and into the other room, where Chyna was fidgeting with her clothes.

For the past couple of months, they had had to lay low. They were sleeping in and operating out of a hotel suite until Chyna received word that the detective who had been following them around had been handled and all his documents confiscated and brought to her.

Chyna felt someone's eyes on her, and she quickly looked back at Sand. "Can you zip this for me?"

Sand knew that she was a major asset to Chyna. With her handling the front line and James handling the dope, Chyna's job was that much easier, and she still got the largest and sweetest piece of the pie.

Sand walked into her office and zipped up the back of Chyna's dress.

"Thanks, Sand. I want to look fashionably presentable for a meeting I have with a very important new client of mine."

Sand stared at Chyna. She was sexy. That couldn't be denied. The way she talked, the way she walked. Everything about her was sexy. But Chyna was fire, and Sand knew it was going to take more than some computer skills and a business degree to do what she needed to do, and that was to beat Chyna at her own game and give payback.

Sand spent the few hours Chyna left her alone thinking about her next move. She had to calculate things carefully if she wanted to make sure Rene stayed safe and unharmed. It was obvious that Chyna was not the only player in this field, and Sand had better be sure she knew everyone's positions, including her own.

At 11:34 p.m., Chyna pulled up in a pearl-white Lexus. She knew from the way Rene was standing that the girl was scared shitless about meeting so late and at such an unusual place. The wind was bone chilling, and while

Rene was trying to keep warm in her thin jacket, Chyna was hotter than grease in a sizzling skillet. One glimpse of Rene and her mind thought nasty thoughts. This was her first time seeing Rene up this close and personal. And if seeing her from a distance did as much as it did for her now, she couldn't wait to see the reaction she would have once she was face-to-face with the young tenderoni. Chyna stepped out of the car nice and slow, throwing her mink on over her dress.

Rene had spotted the Lexus the second it pulled up. She knew then that it had to be the woman she had spoken to over the phone. After seeing her get out of the car, she decided the woman didn't look as threatening as her voice made her seem. But she still couldn't help but think that Chyna had to be messed up in the head to suggest such a crazy place to meet. Rene's guard came down a little. *Hell, what am I scared of?* she thought. Realizing how her hands had been shaking, Rene stuffed them into her pockets. She was no longer petrified, but just in case the bitch was crazy, she gripped a full container of pepper spray, ready to aim and shoot if the situation got out of control.

"Hello. I'm glad you were able to meet with me tonight." Chyna undressed Rene with her eyes. *Damn,* she thought. *Why would such a pretty feminine female want a butch bitch like Sand?*

"Look, half that money is spent, if that's what this is about."

Chyna was still admiring Rene's sexiness. She had to catch herself and remember this was business. "No, no. That's not what this is about. I don't want your money, honey. I just want to ask you a few questions and see if you can help me recover mine. That's all."

Rene looked at Chyna, trying to remember where she had seen her face before.

"You see, Albery owes me for a job he didn't complete. He also owes me for a job he didn't start. Now that his ass is sitting on millions of dollars, he has the nerve to up and retire on me."

Rene was lost and wondered how any of this could involve her. She saw herself as being no help and was curious if Sand had anything to do with this woman coming here, after all.

"I don't think I can help you. . . . Uh, what was your name again?"

Chyna raised her brow a bit. "Some call me Chyndra, but you can call me Chyna."

"Okay, Chyna. As I was saying, I don't think I can help you find what you're looking for."

"I think you can. As a matter of fact, your girl knows you can," Chyna reminded her. She hoped Rene would reflect on the words in the letter that she had written herself and had hand delivered right to her best friend's doorstep.

"What?"

"She assured me that you would be most helpful in assisting me in a timely manner."

Rene looked around, checking her surroundings and listening for any trains. Why did we have to meet up on the railroad tracks? she thought.

"Look, all I need for you to do is make a small transaction. One time is all it would take."

Rene looked back up at Chyna. Chyna saw the uncertainty planted on her face.

"I'll tell you like this, Ma. You do this thing here for me, and you and Sand will be given the best life has to offer. I'll even throw in an incentive." She lifted her brow and batted her eyelashes. "This is a sweet deal, honey," she added, while overworking her brain as she thought about the money she could make off Rene if she joined her team.

Chyna was determined to psyche Rene up. The longer Rene took to answer, the more irritated Chyna grew, as she was hardly giving Rene an option.

Rene thought for a second. "And what would that incentive be?"

Chyna grinned. "That's for me to know and you to find out."

"How much are we talking that he owes you?"

"Let's just say the numbers are up, and it's tax season."

"So, if I do this for you, you'll pay me off and Sand will come back home to me?"

"That's what it is."

Rene stopped for a moment to gather her thoughts. That was what she and Sand needed, a break like this, because she knew the money she had pinched from Johnson and Johnson would take them only so far. Chyna's proposal sounded like it would afford them more security.

"All right. What have I got to lose? The son of a bitch tried to fire me on some bullshit, anyway." This was the perfect revenge, to empty his bank account to a negative zero. She laughed inside at the thought. She remembered the last time she had balanced the books: his company's account had had over six million dollars. What it was like now, she couldn't wait to see. "I'll do it."

"That's my girl. In the meantime, here's a cell phone. It can only receive incoming calls. Only I have the number. I'll contact you when everything is set up. Now, to the right of you, over there under that rock, there's an envelope with your name on it. You can thank me later. Until then, you better get off these tracks. A train is coming." Rene didn't hear a train. Then suddenly the loud sound was banging in her ears.

Choo-chooooo!

She hopped off the tracks so quick, hoping she hadn't peed on herself.

Chyna smiled as she walked back to her car, all the while knowing she had proven her point.

Rene headed for the envelope. She lifted the rock, picked up the envelope, and tore at it eagerly to see what was inside. "Five thousand dollars!" She stuffed the money into her purse and couldn't get in her car fast enough. As she cranked up her engine and drove off, she neglected to notice the red Honda that had been trailing her all week.

To Be Continued in . . .

Stud Princess, Notorious Vendettas.

N'TYSE (pronounced entice [en-tahys])

A former private banker and financial counselor for over twelve years, N'Tyse—a documentarian, philanthropist, and multifaceted hybrid author—is known in the literary world for her evocative prose, taboo story lines, and rambunctious characters. She is a relationship fiction/erotic romance author and editor of several best-selling novels and anthologies, a ghostwriter, literary agent, relationship columnist, and all-purpose blogger.

With a burning hunger to transcend, coupled with her storytelling ingenuity and passion for bringing awareness to cultural issues, N'Tyse dove into the independent filmmaking arena, where she executively produced and directed her first documentary feature, *Beneath My Skin,* which was released in 2014 by her production company, A Million Visions Productions. The film garnered the interest of Maverick Entertainment Group, which eagerly acquired it in 2015 for home video, online streaming, and television distribution.

A Dallas, Texas, native, N'Tyse continues to juggle her writing career with being a full-time mother of two, a wife, and a docu-filmmaker. Her novels include *My Secrets, Your Lies*; *Stud Princess, Notorious Vendettas* (Urban Books/Kensington); *Twisted Seduction*; *Twisted Vows of Seduction*; and *Twisted Entrapment* (Strebor/ Simon & Schuster). She is also the editor of *Gutta Mamis* and *Cougar Cocktales* (Strebor/Simon & Schuster). Her shorter-length works have appeared in *Kontrol Magazine*; *Purple Panties II: Missionary No More*; *Z-Rated: Chocolate Flava 3*; and other publications. Her relationship articles and twisted blog topics can be found on multiple sites where she has featured as a guest blogger. Currently N'Tyse is pursuing film and interdisciplinary research studies at Arizona State University. Her next documentary feature, *Behind the Mask*, is currently in production.

Go beyond the book and connect with the author today!
www.ntyse.com
www.facebook.com/author.ntyse
www.twitter.com/ntyse
Email: ntyse.amillionthoughts@yahoo.com

Watch the hot *Twisted* series trailer by scanning the code below!